CONTENTS

Chapter 36	✻	Trouble	p9
Idle Chat	✻	Celes Strawberries	p55
Chapter 37	✻	My First Errand	p62
Chapter 38	✻	To the Capital	p91
Chapter 39	✻	Negotiations	p115
Chapter 40	✻	Bishop	p155
Chapter 41	✻	Going Home	p169
Extra Story	✻	Mariel's Resolve	p194
Extra Story	✻	Farewell Black Ops!	p199

I Shall Survive Using Potions! Volume 5
by FUNA

Translated by Hiroya Watanabe
Edited by William Haggard
Layout by Leah Waig
English Cover & Lettering by Kelsey Denton

This book is a work of fiction. Names, characters, places, and incidents are the product of the author's imagination or are used fictitiously. Any resemblance to actual events, locales, or persons, living or dead, is coincidental.

Copyright © 2019 FUNA
Illustrations by Sukima

First published in Japan in 2019 by Kodansha Ltd., Tokyo.
Publication rights for this English edition arranged through Kodansha Ltd., Tokyo.

All rights reserved. In accordance with the U.S. Copyright Act of 1976, the scanning, uploading, and electronic sharing of any part of this book without the permission of the publisher is unlawful piracy and theft of the author's intellectual property.

Find more books like this one at www.j-novel.club!

President and Publisher: Samuel Pinansky
Managing Editor (Novels): Aimee Zink
Managing Translator: Kristi Fernandez
QA Manager: Hannah N. Carter
Marketing Manager: Stephanie Hii

ISBN: 978-1-7183-7194-1
Printed in Korea
First Printing: May 2021
10 9 8 7 6 5 4 3 2 1

I SHALL SURVIVE USING POTIONS!

5

Author: FUNA
Illustrator: Sukima

Chapter 36: Trouble

Please contact me right away. -Taona

"What is this?"

Upon returning to our home base, Convenience Store Belle, I was greeted with a piece of paper on the door.

"What could this be about?"

That's a mystery too, but first of all…

"Who's this 'Taona'?"

I had no way of contacting her, since I didn't know who she was. Everyone just cocked their heads in confusion, unsure of who this "Taona" might be.

"Forget it, then!"

Yup, not like there was anything else I could do. I decided to cook up a nice meal and go to bed early tonight. Although I did get to relax at the hot springs, I was pretty tired from everything that had happened, especially the walk home. At that time, the realization still hadn't hit me…

A few days later, when I was talking about our little trip during my visit to Ed and the other horses at the stable, they asked me why I hadn't taken them with me to ride.

"Oh…" I said without thinking, and Ed absolutely flipped out.

"You forgot about us! You completely forgot about us, didn't youuu?!" Ed shouted. I couldn't stand to bear the cold gaze from his wife, along with the look from Roland and Francette's horses, as they were on the verge of tears. I ended up making a bunch of promises and upgrading their meals.

...Damn it.

Though, I really was at fault this time. Guess I had to let it go...

"Why didn't you come see me once you got back?!" Someone came barging in shouting during the afternoon business hours.

"...Do I know you?"

"It's me! Taona!!!"

I cocked my head, then Roland spoke up from behind me.

"She's that old apothecary's disciple!"

"Ah..."

Roland didn't remember her name, but it seemed he recognized her face.

It may not be anything to brag about, but I'm not good at remembering faces... That's really not something to brag about.

In any case, Roland was supposed to be upstairs... When did he sneak up on me like that...?

"So, what does that apothecary's disciple want with me? This shop doesn't handle rare drugs anymore." There was no need to be overly polite with her, considering she wasn't a customer. I was older than her and this wasn't a business relationship, so I didn't have to treat her like a superior.

I had spoken to her with a moody, haughty tone, but then...

"I thought I should let you know that some people who seem to be related to the royal palace and merchants from the royal capital were asking around about you..."

"Thank you so much for coming! Please, go right upstairs! We will prepare some tea and snacks right away..."

Chapter 36: Trouble

Yes, of course I'll treat honored guests with hospitality. That goes without saying!

Taona shot me a look after seeing my attitude do a complete one-eighty, but I didn't care. Information was priceless, even more so when it was free. I didn't mind pandering one bit!

"…So, I decided to warn you, just in case."

I had apologized with some excuse about not being able to see her right away because I didn't know where she lived, then listened to what she had to say. Of course, I wasn't oblivious enough to tell Taona that I didn't know who she was directly to her face.

"…So, those people came to investigate the miracles and strange phenomenon occurring in this city on behalf of their country?" This was bad. But I had already made sure everyone involved was going to keep their mouths shut. My information shouldn't have been leaked…

"Actually, the merchants all seem to have come from different shops, and the ones from the royal palace seem to have been sent here on a personal request. It was as if they were all hired separately by a person who's trying to find you before someone else does. They used phrasing that could be interpreted as if they're working for their government, but it seemed intentionally vague…"

I was impressed by how quick-witted and observant she was, despite her young age. I guess she wasn't an apothecary's disciple for nothing.

"But how did you know they were looking for me?" It shouldn't have been so easy to link me back to my previous selves. Verbal warnings, disguises, threats… I had taken all the proper precautions. I should have been safe here…

"Master Oredeim told them."

"That damn geezerrrrrr! Him again?!" But I had warned him not to tell anyone, too! It didn't seem likely that he would have just spilled the beans…

"Haha, this is a man who blabbed immediately after just a little threat from a baron's retainer. Do you think he would refuse to talk to someone with connections to the royal palace?" Taona said with a disappointed expression.

"Th-Then those merchants are still…"

"Bribes are his weakness, even more so than authority… Ahaha…" Taona laughed weakly. "He isn't a bad person, though…"

"He most definitely is!" I couldn't help but jump in there…

In any case, I was nothing but a little girl who happened to sell some medicine that was kind of rare. And despite that medicine's rarity, it had been sold to the general public, and only once, at that. I even made it a point to say it wouldn't be for sale again. So, this wasn't really that big of a deal, at least when compared to the many miracles I had performed around the same time.

CHAPTER 36: TROUBLE

This thought brought me some relief, until…

"After they heard my master's story, they said, 'We shall go to the house of Baron Dorivell next, whose firstborn son is said to have undergone a miraculous recovery. Then, we will go to Viscount Raphael's stables, where that horse known as Carlos is being kept. Viscount Raphael's servants are unlikely to talk, so we will look for that mysterious little girl who is said to have been buying scrap meat and nuts before the viscount began buying crow food. We will split up and search the meat shop, vegetable shop, and marketplace…'"

"G…"

"G?"

"Gyaaaaaaaaagh!!!"

I took the investigation skills of people in this world too lightly!!!

I didn't think to tell the old man at the stables not to talk to anyone! He had Carlos's sales records and my name and contact information from when I asked him to take care of Ed and the other horses! There are records there that prove definitively that Carlos was mine at the time…

"So they all went around asking for a girl with scary-looking eyes…"

Twitch, twitch

"Oh, nooo! Are you okay, Kaoru?!" I heard Layette's voice in the distance as I fell face-first onto the table and started convulsing…

"…Ah, you're awake!" I awoke to Layette's voice and sat straight up.

"…Where's Taona?"

"She left some time ago." I saw that Francette and Roland had appeared, looking at me with concerned expressions.

Chapter 36: Trouble

Even Francette goes out sometimes. As such, I always make sure to have Roland, or even Emile or Belle, stay with me as my bodyguard. That's why only Layette and Roland had been around earlier. Emile and Belle were off handling jobs from the Hunter's Guild, training and making some money.

"Sir Roland told me everything. It appears this Taona girl understands you quite well.

"After her master told Baron Dorivell about this place, and after he heard about that boy's miraculous recovery, it isn't surprising that she put two and two together, considering the incident with the medicine here and the comment from those men searching for you about the little girl with the scary eyes...

"She may be trying to make amends for her master's actions, but it seems she's on our side. The problem is those men who seemed to have come from the capital. So..." Francette looked at me with a troubled expression. "What shall we do?"

Yeah, what?

...I guess I'll play dumb for now.

It seemed that they were looking for the Angel from Balmore, so I decided to break that down first. I had been known as the Angel for about four years, so most people probably knew what I look like by now, but there weren't too many people who had actually seen me in person, so as long as I could obscure my most notable characteristics, I should be fine.

People who traveled to distant countries were very rare in this world. Even merchants didn't travel that far, for the most part. Unless they were friends with other merchants in those countries, it was far too risky to go somewhere with unknown market conditions. Paying high expenses for transportation, only to find your goods were abundant and cheap there, was a quick way to lose all your money.

So, it was highly unlikely that the people from the capital had seen me in Balmore. Even if they had, I'd be fine if it had just been a glimpse at a distance, all those years ago. And if major characteristics in my appearance were different, they'd probably assume I was someone else entirely.

And so...

"Potion that changes eye and hair color, come out!" I chugged it down right away. Those guys could have appeared at any minute.

I checked myself out in the mirror. Brown hair and hazel eyes.

Good. On top of that...

"Potion container with a black wig on top of it, come out!" I then settled the wig on my head.

Perfect! Since everyone around here already knew I had black hair and brown eyes, I had changed my eyes just enough that I could say they had always been this color, if asked. And for my hair, I could claim I always wore a wig, and my natural hair color was brown.

Many people think Japanese people have black eyes, but they're actually brown. It's a pretty common color on Earth in general. I'd heard that people around Kyushu have hazel eyes, though...

I remembered that, in my past life, there had been a section in my international documents stating my hair and eye color, and they said black hair and brown eyes. I didn't write that myself, mind you. They just handed it to me like that. So, my eyes should still be brown.

I'm told my eyes are black a lot in this world too, but I guess they're more of a blackish-brown.

Anyway, my appearance was good to go. Now I just had to stick to my story!

Chapter 36: Trouble

"Pardon me."

Here we go!

A normal customer wouldn't offer such a greeting upon entering my shop. It was pretty much a declaration stating outright that they weren't a customer. And if it was someone from the palace, they wouldn't have used such a polite and respectful phrase.

Which meant...

"My name is Eridel, a merchant from the capital. Is the owner here, by any chance?" It seemed to be one of the merchants. But why was he alone?

"I am the owner, Quaoru." I fudged up the pronunciation on purpose so it could be plausibly mistaken as "Kaoru." Just so it wouldn't be a flat-out lie...

This way, it would sound like "Quaoru" to this merchant, but people who knew my name would hear it as "Kaoru." Mhm.

The merchant gave me a look of surprise for a moment, but maybe he figured the pronunciation shifted as my name traveled between countries, because he didn't question it. I mean, even if he had, it wasn't like he could argue with me about my own name. I didn't give him some completely different name, because that would only serve to raise suspicion, since he had surely investigated my name already.

That's why I had opted to just change the pronunciation, just a little, within a range that was still believable. He probably wouldn't interpret my name as me denying I was the Angel, but...

"Ahh, Lady Angel! I have come from the capital, representing the Griffon Trading Company, to humbly request to do business with you and your potions..."

"Hold on just a minute!!!" Three men who clearly appeared to be merchants came running into the shop.

"How dare you sneak in without us!"

"We agreed to do the negotiations together!"

"What the hell!!!"

Oh, I see...

"Hm? I have no idea what you're talking about. All business comes down to the merchant's wit and luck. The early bird gets the worm. This is common sense for merchants, no? We are in the middle of a business negotiation. It is against the rules to interject when you arrive late."

"Don't give me that bullshit!" One of the merchants that had just arrived grabbed the Eridel guy by the collar.

"You should know when to quit, Manticore Shop..." Eridel said with an unconcerned smile as his aggressor held him by the collar.

Sheesh, even their shop names sound like they don't get along...

"Now, now, we are all merchants here. Why don't we calm down and talk this out..."

"Yes, Horn Rabbit is right..."

Horn Rabbit? After those two tough-sounding shop names? Oh, I get it. Rabbits — the approachable, fluffy, and tasty rabbit that represents prolificacy and abundance — would make a better name for a shop. Better than a tough-sounding and aggressive one, anyway...

Anyway, I had to sort this situation out.

"Um, so, what could have brought all of you to this humble little shop in a provincial city all the way from the capital?" I asked with a puzzled expression, and the merchants each nodded as if they understood.

Damn, they must have investigated everything about me already...

Chapter 36: Trouble

"What's going on, Quaoru?" Belle asked as she came downstairs. Earlier, I had pressed the button to signal for her to come down and act normal.

...Francette was with her too.

Why, Francette...? I didn't call for you...

Unlike the lightly-dressed Belle, Francette stood out like a sore thumb, fully clad as she was in heavy armor in a small shop like this...

Yup, the merchants were all nodding, as if they had expected this.

"Belle, watch the counter for me. And you take them upstairs, please," I asked Belle and Francette, respectively, and everyone but Belle went up to the second floor.

I didn't call Francette by her name because Fearsome Fran was extremely famous in Balmore and was known to be very close to the Angel. That's also why I didn't call Roland by his name either, of course. I was only able to call Emile, Belle, and Layette by their names in front of the merchants or anyone from the royal palace.

The four merchants sat next to each other in a row, and I sat alone on the opposite end. Francette stood behind me and to the side, so she could attack the men at any time, if they tried anything funny.

Roland had a bit too much of a noble aura, right down to his equipment, so I had him wait in the next room over with Emile. Francette alone would be considered overkill for dealing with just four merchants. I could probably even kick one of these fatsos out myself, if it came down to it.

"Umm, I don't quite get what's going on, but I'm guessing you all want to purchase products from me?"

"Yes!" As I thought, it seemed they wanted to gain my favor and some healing potions...

"Then please feel free to buy whatever is on the shelves downstairs..."

"No, no, no, no!"

Wow, they're perfectly synced.

They had been at each other's throats earlier, but maybe they were actually close friends...

"So you're saying you want something other than what we sell in the shop?"

Nod, nod, nod, nod.

"Hmm, it'd be a pain to manage the same items through multiple different distributors, so it might be better to have one shop handle it all..." The air turned extremely tense as soon as the words left my mouth. So much so that Francette put a hand to her sword hilt without thinking about it.

I also heard a noise from next door, which I figured was Emile, as untrained as he was, inadvertently making noise as he stood up from his chair in response.

But man, these merchants... A bit too intense, don't you think?

Now that I had them pitted against each other again...

"First, I can say that anyone who betrays the allies they've been working with can't be trusted to do business with. Who knows when I'd be betrayed, too..."

"What!" Eridel's eyes widened in shock, and the other three merchants smirked, as if to say he deserved it.

Then...

"As for you, you resorted to violence rather than negotiations and words, despite being a merchant. If you decide to use violence to force me into a deal that's favorable for you, a little girl like me wouldn't be able to do anything about it, so I will have to pass..."

Chapter 36: Trouble

I directed my words to the owner of Manticore Shop, and his eyes also widened as if he couldn't believe what he had heard.

"Wha…"

The fact that he was surprised was more surprising to me, to be honest. Did he really think a woman would feel safe working with someone who saw no problem with trying to make his competitor comply through violence in front of a potential new business partner?

"Manticore Shop" glared daggers at Eridel, as if to say it was his fault. There were smiles on the two remaining merchants' faces.

All right, next…

"Now, who should I do business with…" The eager spirit emanating from the two was palpable.

Then…

"The intensity in here is scaring me… This doesn't feel like the right time to talk business, so would you mind postponing for now? Whatever is going on between the four of you doesn't really concern me, and this is all a bit too much… Perhaps once you've figured this out among yourselves, one of you can come by again to discuss this further…"

The merchants looked at each other, then seemed to realize there was no point in arguing and agreed to leave for now.

"…We will see you again tomorrow, then…"

With that, they left. They really didn't need to come back, though.

Anyway, this was enough for today. They might be back tomorrow, but it would probably just be one of them. There was no way the merchants would agree to let just one of them have exclusive rights to the business, so one of them would probably come as a representative to distribute the products among the other three.

I wonder what kind of products they want to stock, though...

What could be worth traveling out to a provincial city like this, paying the fees for transportation and security, and bringing them all the way back to the royal capital?

I mean, I never claimed to be the Angel, and even if I was, I didn't agree to sell them any potions. Besides, what made them think I'd sell products to other merchants when they're not even for sale in my own store? I decided to offer some cookies I baked, a wooden animal Emile had carved, and some bamboo wares that Belle had made to whoever came back representing the other merchants. These were the best deals in my shop. The materials were cheap and we just made them for fun, so they were super affordable.

Francette tried dipping her toes into handicrafts, too.

...She's probably better off sticking to swordsmanship.

"Pardon me!" The next day, one of the merchants from yesterday came by during the morning business hours. It was one of the merchants who hadn't been involved in that little grappling session, the one who wasn't the owner of Horn Rabbit. Come to think of it, I never got his shop name.

"I am Latton of the Solcus Trading Company."

So he's the one who's gonna handle the negotiations.

I figured the guy who tried to screw the others over and the violent one were both out of the question, so there were only two options left anyway.

"Please join me upstairs." I flipped the sign at the entrance to indicate that we were closed, locked the door, and guided him to the second floor.

It was just me and Francette again. There was no way she wouldn't be present when I was meeting with someone. You never knew what could happen, according to her.

Chapter 36: Trouble

I mean, she's right, so I let her do her thing.

"So, the product you're looking to buy from my shop…"

"Your potions, of course! The legendary potions that you sold in the kingdom of Balmore!"

Figures… But.

"Oh, like liquid medicine? We only have the kind that's used for relieving throat pain and cleaning wounds. They're both one silver coin for a small bottle each…"

"Huh? A-Are they magical medicine blessed by the Goddess with miraculous effects…?"

"No, just normal medicine. It's not too different from the kind you can buy at any apothecary, so the bottles are priced about the same. It may be cheaper to buy them from your local apothecary when you consider the transportation fees and such."

"…" Oh, he seemed rather troubled.

"U-Um, Miss Angel, about the ones you had been selling at Balmore…" Latton looked at me as if I was playing dumb and holding out on the good stuff. Well…

"Excuse me, but who is this 'Angel' you're referring to? And I don't understand why you're so fixated on a small shop like this…"

"What? Oh, no, there's no need to hide it. We already know the details of what had transpired… The fact that you've been active as the Angel in Balmore, how you saved Baron Dorivell's son, how you helped the house of Viscount Raphael, everything. Your black hair and black eyes are undeniable proof…"

There! That's my cue!

"What? I'm not this Angel you're talking about. I could even swear it to the Goddess herself."

"Huh?" He looked at me, dumbfounded.

I guess it wasn't too surprising, considering his conviction that I was the Angel and I had flatly denied it. But, for the record, I'd been denying that title ever since I had reincarnated in this world. They kept calling me that no matter how many times I denied it, so I gave up on actually trying to stop it, but I never claimed to be one myself. So this wasn't actually a lie.

And to finish it off…

"Besides, I don't have black hair and black eyes. My eyes may be dark, but they're actually brown. See? Look carefully." I brought my face closer to his, and he carefully stared into my eyes.

"…You're right… Not only are they not black, they're not even a black-brown. They're more like hazel…" The merchant was dumbstruck.

I pressed on.

"And about my hair…" I grasped my wig and pulled it off my head.

"I wear this wig because I like the look. It's not my real hair. As you can see, my natural hair color is brown…" *Ah, he turned to stone.*

"Wh-Wh-Wha..." He regained his composure a few seconds later and managed to stammer.

"Y-You tricked me!"

I most definitely did NOT.

"Tricked you? I had no idea what you were talking about from the beginning... I never once claimed to be this Angel you spoke of, and you all went on about who-knows-what without a proper explanation. I'm still not entirely sure what's going on..."

The merchant finally seemed to realize he was at fault and grew quiet. Then...

"I-I'll be leaving! Sorry for the trouble." He gave a half-hearted apology and quickly retreated.

"Amazing, Kaoru! I could never hope to deceive and entrap people as expertly as you!" Francette said.

"Is that supposed to be a compliment?!"

And so, things had been resolved for now.

...Next, I had to deal with the folks from the royal palace.

"May I speak to the shop owner, please!" The next person to come in wasn't someone from the royal palace at all.

"M-Mariel? How did you..." It was Viscountess Mariel von Raphael, the owner of Carlos and current head of the Raphael household.

I had never told her my real name or identity, and I definitely hadn't told her where I was staying. So, in Mariel's mind, she should know me as the goddess who's friends with Celestine, who had descended to the mortal realm just to help them...

There was no way she could know I was here.

Could it be a coincidence? Or maybe she had some other business here? But what could the head of a noble house want with a commoner's little shop like this?

CHAPTER 36: TROUBLE

I stood there frozen and unable to understand the reason for her visit, and then...

"Excuse me, miss, is the shop owner here by any chance?"

Huh? My disguise isn't that *convincing, is it?*

I mean, sure, I had changed my hair and eye color back then, but my chestnut hair turning black wasn't something that would drastically change my appearance like blonde or silver hair did. My eyes had undergone a pretty big change from blue to hazel, but it wasn't dramatic enough to turn me into a completely different person.

My skin was lighter, too, but getting a bit tan wouldn't make me unrecognizable. Such minor changes couldn't possibly be enough to make me seem like someone else...

I mean, when I ran into Francette the second time, I had silver hair and different colored eyes. Plus, she recognized me instantly, even though there was no way she was expecting to see a goddess walking around in town.

Wait a minute...

I made fists with both hands and stuck out my pointer fingers. Then I pressed a finger from each hand on the edges of my eyes and drooped them downward.

"Ah, Lady Goddess!"

I knew it! Damn it!

Afterward, I flipped the sign at the door to show that we were closed, then drew the curtains and moved upstairs. I had to hear Mariel out before anything else.

Francette, Belle, and Layette joined our meeting. Mariel was a young lady who had been raised in seclusion, so being around strange men might have made her nervous. The guys were probably in the room next door with their ears to the wall. The walls were paper-thin here, so you could hear everything.

Mariel was a viscountess, but she thought I was a goddess, and I didn't feel like putting in the effort to speak all proper, so I decided to play it casually.

"I came to warn you! Merchants, from the capital!"

Yup, I knew that.

"Not only that, but some men who seem to be working for the royal palace have arrived!"

Yup, I knew that.

"And they seem to be looking for a girl with scary... eyes..."

Yup, I knew that too. Mariel carefully studied my face.

"...They were talking about you, Goddess..."

Yup.

In any case, there was one thing I wanted to know.

"How did you know I was here?"

Where was the leak? I had to track it down and plug it up. This was of the highest priority. I stared at Mariel, then...

"Oh, I asked my dogs."

"Hwaa?" I couldn't help but let out a pathetic noise.

"Um, my dogs, they told me... Goddess—"

"Wait, hold up! Can we stop with that Goddess thing? Who knows who might hear you, and if you get used to calling me that, you might let it slip at inconvenient times."

Chapter 36: Trouble

"Ah..." It seemed she understood.

"Call me Kaoru..."

"Yes, of course!"

There was no point in going by Quaoru with Mariel. Besides, she'd probably hear Francette and the others call me Kaoru anyway.

According to Mariel, she had asked the dogs at her house if they knew where I was, and they led her to the place where I fed the dogs and crows, then tracked me to my location. The dogs told her they could have tracked my scent from the viscount's manor, but this way was faster...

Damn, they had some fine noses. Guess that's to be expected of dogs.

The shop was already closed by the time they had arrived, so she decided to go home and come back another day. And here we were.

"Ahhh! Now that you mention it, I forgot to tell the dogs and crows to keep their mouths shut! I mean, I didn't expect that you'd end up being able to talk to animals, and who could've guessed they would spill the beans on my location?!" My original plan was to give Carlos the ability to speak human language. But Mariel requested to be able to speak to animals herself, so I ended up shifting gears to that instead.

I was convinced by Mariel's reasoning that it would be much easier for her to support stray dogs and crows, and to help her keep her promise of helping them one time each when they were injured or sick. It was a sudden change in plans, so I hadn't thought about all the implications...

Well, that was my bad. No point thinking about it now. There was still one important thing I needed to confirm.

"Mariel, could you have been followed on the way here?"

Mariel replied to my question with a serious expression.

"Nothing is absolute, so I can't say the possibility is zero. However, I believe it's very unlikely that anyone would have trailed me here...

"I snuck out of the manor through the back entrance in plain, unassuming clothing, stayed in a room at a shop that I had made arrangements with beforehand, then switched outfits with a maid I had staying there, who is of a height and hair color similar to me. I exited through the back door of that shop some time after that maid left.

"Then I repeated similar diversionary tactics two more times. Afterward, I slipped through crowded main streets quite aggressively, moving against the flow of foot traffic, and used other methods to throw off anyone who could have been pursuing me. Even someone who was highly experienced at trailing someone would likely have lost me."

...Just who the heck are you, Mariel?!

She had taken maneuvers to throw off pursuers who may or may not have been there with expert execution.

"Well, if you went through all that, I think we should be fine this time. It might be risky if you keep doing it, though. Next time you want to contact me, have a maid who looks like a young underservant come buy something at my shop."

"Y-Yes, of course."

I couldn't deny the possibility of someone who wanted connections with a goddess watching Mariel, in case she got in contact with me. And if she pulled the same trick a few times, it would become much easier for them to notice.

As soon as they found out she was trying to lose them, it'd be over. It would be admitting that she knew someone was trying to

Chapter 36: Trouble

track her and she was deliberately trying to lose them, which would be a dead giveaway that she was hiding something.

If a professional realized this, we'd be left with few options. A professional who doesn't mind putting the necessary manpower, effort, and funds into tracking someone down couldn't be stopped by an amateur, no matter how hard she tried.

So, the important thing was to avoid suspicion in the first place. That was why she should use a young girl, a lesser servant, rather than a close, trusted subordinate. As long as we knew she wouldn't betray us, all we needed her to do was deliver letters.

And I doubt there was anyone in this world who would betray the Goddess... Not anyone who knows about Celes's past, anyway.

So, that's that.

The rest of what Mariel told me was just as I had heard from the apothecary's disciple, Taona. The house of Viscount Raphael never leaked anything, so there was no new information there.

Now, all I had to do was deal with the people from the palace...

"Shall I dispose of the palace's men?"

Bffft! H-How did we get there?

"Sniffing around your business is blasphemy, Goddess. If you so desire, I can take care of it tonight..."

Hold up.

Wait, wait, wait.

Wait, wait, wait, wait, wait!

What's gotten into you, Mariel?!

"There's no need to worry. Their actions told me they were working with the kingdom, but they were very deliberate in their word choice. They may be working under orders directly from someone around the royal palace, but those orders are from an individual operating independently rather than being official.

"So, if they did go missing and the incident was to be investigated, the fact that they were acting as though under official mandate and as if someone had directed them to do so would become quickly evident. Someone would very much be troubled by this going public, so they would likely make sure no one found out…"

Hm, she came to the same conclusion as Taona. They were both sharp girls, after all. Give them the same information to analyze and they get to the same destination…

Hold on, this solution is way scarier!

"When you say 'dispose,' do you mean you're gonna ask those Black Ops people?"

Black Ops… A dark, illegal organization that had taken the lives of Mariel's family.

"No, they've mostly been dismantled. The remaining few are currently being hunted down. The only ones left are the weak ones, so they're all but powerless now."

Huh?

"H-H-How…" I did understand why Mariel would hate the Black Ops for carrying out the murder of her parents. But this was an underground crime syndicate that even the count, who was the head of her parent house, hadn't been able to do anything about. How did she pull it off…?

Mariel, your smile is scaring me…

Even Francette was getting weirded out. Could she be going the same route as Emile, Belle, and Francette?

"I used my army."

"Huh?"

It couldn't be. This wasn't Viscount Raphael's domain. It was their neighboring parent house's territory, Count Maslias's domain.

Chapter 36: Trouble

Viscount Maslias's domain was rather small and contained no major cities, so even though their principal residence was located in the capital territory (however remote of an area it might be), they spent most of the year living in a villa in Count Maslias's territory. Now was one of those times.

It was much more convenient to live in and do politics this way. According to her, their own domain was small enough to just leave it to her trusted retainers to handle.

Since they were neighboring territories, with their respective capitals located close to each other, she could go check on her own domain at any time while staying in the count's domain, and a retainer or an emissary could come see her whenever an issue came up.

So, my point is...

There was no way she could mobilize her soldiers freely in a domain other than her own; particularly if it belonged to a parent house that outranked her. Even if she had notified him that she had no intention of raising a rebellion, there was no way that would fly. It was basically saying, "You don't have the ability to take care of this issue yourself, so I'll do it for you," and then moving your army into their territory.

It would be one thing if a parent house did so to a house under them, but the other way around was unheard of. Besides, it didn't seem possible for a viscount house's army to take out the Black Ops so quickly when the count hadn't been able to oppose them all this time.

Something didn't add up. There was definitely something going on here.

...But I was too scared to ask for any further details.

I listened to Mariel for some time after, then we called it a day. She made a face like it was the end of the world when I told her not to come back in person, so as to stay inconspicuous about our making contact, but it couldn't be helped. I thought I heard her make some dangerous comments about having to eliminate them all, but I decided not to think about it. It was better for my mental health not to. Besides, thinking about it wouldn't have solved anything.

"Wh-What should we do, Kaoru…?" Francette asked after Mariel left, but the answer was obvious.

"Well, nothing."

"Huh…?"

There was no need for me to do anything, really.

"I'm just a cute little girl who owns a shop. I have nothing to worry about, right?"

"…" Roland and Emile came over from the next room to join Francette and Belle.

Why are you all staring at me like that?! Layette's the only one on my side here! Damn it…

Chapter 36: Trouble

"In any case, all those incidents have absolutely nothing to do with me. The Angel from Balmore has different-colored hair and eyes, and I don't sell any potions. I'm just your run-of-the-mill general goods store owner with slightly non-standard business hours and products."

"Y-Yes, but…" Francette didn't sound convinced. She probably figured someone sent from the royal palace wouldn't be fooled or back down so easily.

"Well, there's some distance between here and the capital, so it should take at least several days for them to get back to the capital, make their report, figure out the next move, then come back here again.

"The information that actually gets to them will be incomplete or downright wrong, anyway, since they would only hear whatever the messengers tell them based on limited information and their own conjecture.

"And even if something does go down, we just have to get out of here before the message gets to the capital and they send someone here to make a move.

"If we travel along the coastline from here, we could easily cross the eastern border before any pursuers arrive. We have our horses and the chariot, after all."

Thanks to the Item Box, it would only take a few minutes to pack everything in the shop. I'd give Ed and the horses a little boost with my potions, too. And by using the chariot and Item Box, I could throw off any pursuers by changing our setup from a group of five riders to a group consisting of a chariot with four riders to escort it. It was perfect!

"I'm glad I chose a city by the sea instead of the capital. Events that would take half a day in the capital take half a month to a whole month here, so I can really spread my wings."

Having so much physical distance between us and those in power was a significant defensive advantage. Provincial cities like this one weren't very densely populated, so business wasn't as good, but I wasn't concerned about that. The seafood here was nice and fresh with the sea being so close too.

Even with my Item Box's ability to keep things in stasis, it was pointless if the food was already a day old at the time I bought it.

Now I just have to deal with the royal palace (or someone connected to them in some way)! Different hair and eye color, check! Black wig, check! And I told Francette not to come down until I called for her, no matter what. I made sure that she would stay in her room until I specifically called for her, even when I brought the guest upstairs. Okay, good! Ready to go!

"Is the owner here?!"

Here we go...

A normal customer wouldn't say something like that upon entering a shop. That meant only one thing...

"Hm? Are you the shop owner?" He said it after staring right at my face.

This jerk thinks I have scary-looking eyes...!

Well, whatever.

But he was acting awfully haughty for someone who thought I was the Angel. Maybe he didn't know? Or it could be that he'd heard about it but didn't believe it. He probably thought it was some sort of mistake or even a scam. Either that, or just a little brat who was being put on a pedestal by gullible people.

I mean, if I really was an angel, I probably wouldn't have left the country to run a dingy little shop in some other place. The higher-ups probably wouldn't have let that pass. He probably assumed that was something I would do if I had been a fraud who fled the country in a hurry for fear of getting exposed. And the role of people like him was to filter out the facts, so they wouldn't move into the next step until later. The only information they had at this point was probably just Mariel's and the count's reports.

Some merchants and people in positions of power who were quick to pick up on information may have heard about the Longevity Potion incident or the baron's son, but that was about it. So the main target of this investigation was Mariel, and I was probably just a bonus that appeared on the radar when they arrived here.

Considering he got to me so much later than the merchants, maybe he wasn't putting in too much effort... No, that couldn't be right. They'd be in big trouble if they didn't meet their boss's expectations. It would be even worse if word got out that the merchants got to me first. The merchants were just more capable and more sensitive to information, was all.

Maybe he demanded information from the merchants and they sent him my way assuming I was a miss... Without mentioning that I wasn't who they were looking for, of course.

Yeah, they probably left that part out so it technically wasn't a full-on lie. That was just what merchants did. Even if they didn't lie, it didn't mean they were being honest.

This was a group of three consisting of a self-important bureaucrat type and two of his subordinates. The subordinates didn't seem like fighters. Maybe they were just attendants and there to keep in contact with the capital? Either way, it looked like I would just be dealing with the main guy.

"Yes, I am the owner." I only answered the specific question that was asked. There was no need for me to offer more information than needed. These weren't my guests. I had no obligation to provide them with any information for free. Particularly when such information could be used against me.

It takes proper skill and compensation to get good information out of someone, but it didn't seem like this guy understood that. He probably thought I'd tell him anything he wanted if he just raised his voice and barked orders at me.

"What is your name?"

"My mother always told me not to give my name out to strangers…"

"Huh?" The bureaucrat-looking guy looked dumbfounded. …I'll just refer to him as Bureaucrat.

My words finally seemed to register, and his face turned red as he began to shout.

"Y-You! Do you know who I am?!"

"No, I don't. All I know is you barged in here without so much as introducing yourself, demanded I give up some personal information, then started yelling and trying to intimidate me." I then rang the handbell on the counter.

thud thud thud thud thud thud thud!

"Is it a robber? It must be a robber. It's a robber!!!"

"Wh-Wha…"

Emile shouted as he came running down the stairs, Belle following closely behind him.

Bureaucrat and his subordinates had a look of panic as they heard the two rushing down. Emile had shouted at the top of his lungs, so his voice carried outside the shop, attracting a crowd around the building.

Yeah, my response was going to change based on how they acted. That went without saying. That was why I had prepared several patterns for Emile's response based on how I rang the bell. This one told him to treat them like robbers and make a scene.

It was mainly me and Layette watching the shop, so the locals thought I was a hard-working kid taking care of my little sister and treated us well. Apparently, they thought Emile and Belle were my brother and his lover, who contributed to the family's finances by doing hunter work and helping around the shop.

As for Francette and Roland, they were seen as parasites who just wandered around doing nothing, leeching off the children's earnings. Since no one had seen them working, covering at the shop, or going out on errands, they looked like a couple of bums. They didn't work as hunters despite their fancy-looking equipment, and they didn't even hold the bags for the children when they went shopping together. They just went along on the walk for the sake of walking.

Supposedly, their good looks made their scumminess stand out all the more... Not too great of a reputation. Though, the duo in question had no idea that others saw them that way. Not to mention, they were pretty popular among those other than the locals here, like store employees and people they met on the street...

I mean, they didn't help carry things because they had to have both hands free, so they could draw their swords immediately in the event of an ambush. I couldn't really blame them for that...

But other than that, whenever we all went out to eat, Francette ate several times more than a normal adult woman, and Roland was an ex-prince, so he'd order expensive things without so much as a second glance.

...And I'm the one who pays.

Well, it'd be a pain for the staff to have us pay separately, and I wasn't confident in Roland's ability to handle money on his own anyway, considering he had never paid for anything himself before going on this journey. Roland and Francette didn't want to have me pay for all of their living expenses, of course, so they did reimburse me in gold coins every week.

But since the locals didn't know about any of this, they only saw that the kids were the only ones working, and that Layette and I didn't eat much. Besides, Emile, Belle, Layette, and I were used to being poor, so we always picked the affordable options at eateries and stores. Unlike Roland and Francette, who didn't even look at prices... It was no wonder people had such bad impressions of them.

Although Francette was born a commoner, she was now a noble and tried not to embarrass her country or Roland by not acting the part, so she ordered the same things as Roland, making her seem like a frivolous spender.

Plus, whenever Layette and I went out, it was for stocking products, buying food at the market, and showing up at the Commerce Guild, while Emile and Belle went out to the Hunter's Guild. Meanwhile, Roland and Francette went out to fancy restaurants and taverns where rich folks hung out.

It wasn't like the brother of a king could escort his aristocrat fiancée to a cheap restaurant or tavern. Besides, if those two went to such a place, someone would try to start something with them.

...But, oh well. There was nothing I could do about it.

If they were happy and didn't notice what was going on, I was fine with it. Don't fret over the small stuff! So, in any case, if Layette, Emile, Belle, or I found ourselves in danger, the neighbors would come flying in to help us. ...Like they were now.

"What the hell are you doing?! Hey, someone call the guards!" A crowd had gathered around the door, some of them marching into the shop to shout at Bureaucrat's crew.

They hadn't actually laid a hand on me and looked fairly respectable in appearance, so the locals didn't come in swinging or hold them down by force, but tensions were running pretty high. The people here seemed to think I was only twelve years old or so, and Layette, who was sitting on my lap, was actually only six. It seemed the locals considered me to be one of them, considering they went at Bureaucrat's group with so much aggression despite him obviously holding some position of power. It was pretty touching…

"Wait! This isn't what you think! We are emissaries on a mission from the capital!" They could have spouted some parting remark and fled, but if they had, they wouldn't have been able to come back. Such an exit would mean guaranteed trouble the next time one of the locals saw them, and it would have been over for them if I screamed the next time they returned.

So, in order for them to have a discussion with me, they had to dispel any misunderstandings here and now. They desperately tried to get a word in, but I wasn't letting them off so easily.

"Oh? Is an emissary's job to barge into a shop and suddenly start shouting demands without even naming yourself or explaining what you're here for?"

"Huh…?"

"And whose orders are you here on, anyway? What exactly did they tell you to do, and were you instructed to bully children without stating your own name or position? I have nothing to say to you unless you give us the name of your employer."

"Uh…"

"…"

He couldn't just reveal the person who had given him his orders in front of such a big crowd. They had probably made a move in the hope of getting ahead of other authority figures and people related to the royal palace, and it would be hard to give out a name after I had called him out on his aggressive behavior and lack of common sense.

And he didn't seem to realize it, but I was deliberately phrasing things in a way that would make people get the wrong idea about his intentions. It wasn't a lie, though.

This man knew his own objective, of course, so he realized my comments were related. But from the perspective of someone who didn't know what we were talking about…

"You've got some nerve, trying to put your hands on a child… And your boss is a criminal, hiring a bunch of thugs to kidnap someone! Who the hell gave you your orders?! Spit it out, or else…" These men were just an emissary and his attendants, and the two subordinates weren't necessarily his guards or anything. In other words, they were gonna be useless in a fight.

They were outnumbered by the locals, some of which looked pretty tough. Not to mention they were against Emile, who was armed with a sword, and Belle, who had a dagger.

Good, they looked troubled…

"You've been claiming you came from the capital and that you're emissaries, but it's possible that you were sent by a crime boss from the capital to kidnap some kids. It's completely pointless and doesn't put my mind at ease at all when you just tell us you're an emissary from the capital without giving us your employer's name or why you're here. We don't even know if what you say is true…"

"Wha…" Bureaucrat stumbled over his words for a moment; then, just as he prepared to yell at me again, he noticed the look from Emile, the younger man gripping the hilt of his weapon, as well as the glares from the locals, and shut his mouth.

"In any case, I've never been to the capital, I have no family there, and I don't know anyone from there who might have any business with me. The only possibility I can think of is that some scoundrel noticed me and decided to kidnap me, or enslave me, or try to threaten me and take my shop by force."

Chapter 36: Trouble

"Wh-What are you..." His eyes widened at my words. But I wasn't saying anything outrageous or anything. The looks in the locals' eyes were getting pretty scary now...

Then, as this went on...

"Hey, I brought an officer!" One of the local guys brought over a local law enforcement type who seemed to be in his mid-twenties.

Though, this wasn't the capital, so this wasn't some powerful elite soldier. He was just an average low-ranking guy who might have trained a bit. At the same time, he was a resident of the city and he knew everyone.

...In other words, he would prioritize protecting someone who lived here over the desires of strangers. Especially when we're talking about a trio of strangers who were displaying inexcusable behavior and threatening some (seemingly) underage girls.

"So you're the maggots who banded together and barged into the shop to threaten some children?!"

Whoa, he really hit the ground running there!

I noticed the officer glancing to one side, then saw that he was looking at a girl in the crowd who seemed to be seventeen or eighteen years old. Aha... So he was plotting to show off for that young girl.

Well, it was more convenient for me the more dramatic he got with it.

"Wh-What are you saying? I am here from the capital..."

"That's all he's been saying this whole time, refusing to give us his name, his employer's name, or why he's here. He doesn't even know my name, either. That leaves only one explanation..."

They really hadn't given any names yet. He should have just said his and his employer's name, along with why he was here, but he underestimated me because I was a little girl and decided to start shouting and demanding answers.

He would have a hard time giving those names out in front of this crowd and officer now. If he did, rumors would spread like wildfire. So the more authority his employer had, the harder it would be to name him now. He'd have to be taken into custody by the officer, then prove his innocence by giving out the names where no one else was around. ...If he could prove it, that is.

"Y-You..." Bureaucrat gave me a death glare, then turned to the officer and spoke. "I am here on orders from the royal palace. Do you realize what will happen if you defy me?!"

The officer looked unfazed.

"...Do you have any way to prove your claim?"

"These two will testify!" With that, he pointed at his two companions.

But the officer just shrugged in response.

"...And do you have proof that *they're* associated with the royal palace?"

"Huh...?"

I mean, he should have expected that...

"Argh, do you understand the consequences you will face later?!"

Chapter 36: Trouble

"Well, if I let some criminal go just because he claimed to have a position of authority without any proof, I'd get fired. And even if you really are someone of high standing, I would only get praised for arresting you at the scene of the crime, not reprimanded. This city isn't so rotten that we let criminals go just because they hold positions of power."

"What…?"

Whoa, the people here actually had morals! Though, the crimes he spoke of were just threatening me and attempting to make me do as he demanded. It may have just been an argument between a customer and worker if I had been male, but since I was a woman… or rather, since I looked like an underage girl…the phrasing from that earlier conversation made it sound like he had tried to commit a much more serious crime.

I mean, he did try to make me tell him things by force and take me to the capital, so it wasn't entirely wrong.

In any case, enjoy your visit to the station! Since it was only a failed attempt and he seemed to hold some position of authority, he'd probably just end up getting scolded by the officer and his superiors.

I doubted he would get thrown in jail when he hadn't actually laid hands on me. Maybe he'd get a warning to stay away from me from now on.

Oh, I know!

"Excuse me, can you have him come closer to me?"

"Hm? Oh, sure…" With that, the officer cautiously told Bureaucrat's group to walk closer to me.

"Can you look into my eyes?"

"Huh? O-Okay then…" With that, Bureaucrat moved his face closer to mine.

"Th-They're hazel..." He looked dumbfounded. So he did think I had black hair and black eyes. Naturally, that also meant he knew about the Angel.

"And..." I lifted the wig off of my head.

"B-Brown hair?!"

There, that should have nailed the idea that I wasn't the so-called Angel of Balmore into his head. ...Though, I never actually claimed such a title at all.

He must have heard from that loose-lipped apothecary. Or maybe he heard about the Viscount Raphael incident and followed the trail from their stable. It was even possible that he heard it from those other merchants from the capital.

Whatever the case, I was just a clerk at this small-time shop who had no connection to the Angel of Balmore, the Raphael household, or the miracle at Baron Dorivell's house. He should have believed that at this point.

And for the final blow...

"Oh, wait, did you get duped by someone like those merchants? They kept going on about black hair and black eyes, so I showed them my real eye and hair color, and they left immediately. That's why I just showed you the same thing."

"Wha..."

There! Mission accomplished! There was now no doubting that I was completely unrelated to those incidents, and I just happened to sell some herbs to that geezer. I had nothing to do with Viscount Raphael's household, and I didn't know any Baron Dorivell.

What's that? The stable? There weren't many pastures in the suburbs with stables that also took care of horses. I just so happened to leave my horses at House Raphael's stables by coincidence.

Chapter 36: Trouble

…I mean, that was true.

If anyone looked into the time when I arrived at the city and left Ed and the others at the stables, it would be clear that we had no prior relation. Besides, there was no reason for me to leave my horses at the same stables and risk getting unwanted attention.

Bureaucrat and his entourage should refrain from showing their faces here now. If they did, they'd get thrown in jail for sure.

And since there was no way he could tell his employer that he had failed to get in contact with me, give me his employer's name, or explain what he wanted with me because of his arrogant attitude, all of this wouldn't be included in his report.

He probably knew about the Angel of Balmore already but found out about me after he had arrived in this city. Since I was just something that came up along the way of his investigation, or maybe he had heard about me from the merchants, there was no need to report on me at all.

Plus, I was sure he thought of me as an annoying brat who only brought trouble.

…And so, Bureaucrat and his crew were taken away by the officer.

There, it was all taken care of.

My peaceful, leisurely life would come back again, starting tomorrow. Good, good…

The day after I had successfully fended off the group from the capital… After finishing my morning work, I had left to go to the market. On the way there, since I was already out and about, I took a slight detour to Mariel's place, House Raphael's estate in Viscountess Mariel's domain.

I just felt like it, no particular reason. The chances of her being outside and us seeing each other were pretty much none. It wasn't like a viscountess would be tending to her garden or sweeping the front of the gate by herself.

Huh? Is that...

When I turned the corner and the manor came into play, I noticed something next to the gate...

A dog? Two dogs sat there, one on each side, like guardians of the gate. And similarly, two hawks perched atop the pillars on either side, as well as two pigeons beside them.

Yeah, it might not be a good look if they were crows... Wait, that's not the issue here!

"Oh, is this your first time here? That's the manor of the noble lady Viscountess Raphael, who has received the blessing of the Goddess. That's why those dogs and birds, which are servants of the Goddess, are protecting it."

An old man passing by explained this all to me as I stood there, mouth agape.

"Whaaat..."

I thought the deal was that she would help them once in case they got injured or sick...

And why were there birds other than crows, ones that had nothing to do with that incident...?

I understood the first half of what the old man was saying. After that whole show we put on in front of such a crowd, it only made sense.

But what was with the latter half?! How did this happen...?

"That's why we all call her... the Bitch Viscountess."

"Whaaaaaat?!" That sounds incredibly offensive...

At least I thought so for a second. But come to think of it, the terms for genders used in people and animals were the same. They both used "female."

So the title was meant to mean "the viscount protected by dog servants," which was shortened to "Dog Viscount," and since she was a woman, or in other words, a viscountess, they just added "lady" to make it "Lady Dog Viscountess."

The auto-translation function in my brain just recognized "female dog" as "bitch" since the words were arranged that way.

…Why wouldn't it be "the Viscountess of Dogs" or something?! Well, I guess that made it sound like she was a dog herself, so it wasn't much different…"

"Oh, there've been orders to stop using that nickname," a young man who happened to be walking by said after overhearing our conversation.

Yeah, that made sense. That name was a bit much…

"We all call her the Bird Aristocrat now." They couldn't think of anything better…?

CHAPTER 36: TROUBLE

I approached the gate after the two men left.

"Hey, why are you here?" I asked in a whisper…to the dog.

"Ah, Lady Goddess! Thank you so much for introducing me to such a fine job. Since that incident, I've been employed by Lady Mariel for other matters. Many of my friends are now serving her. Watching the gates in shifts, lying about the building and keeping an eye out for intruders.

"And it hasn't occurred as of late, but there are times when we are summoned to handle some…rougher matters."

"The attack on the Black Ops!!!" The mystery was solved. So that's what happened…

"What about the crows?"

"The crows were, um, rather intimidating, so they're working behind the scenes. The new hires are more visually appealing, so they're usually given the more public roles."

"I…I see. I'm happy that you got a nice job. Well, see you around…"

"Yes, if you need anything, please don't hesitate to ask. We will come to your aid at any time!"

…Mariel was more capable than I thought. And she was pretty crafty…

Though, since the Black Ops were the ones who killed her parents and brother for money, she had a vendetta against them alongside the one with her uncle Aragorn. And they were a crime ring that had been giving Count Maslias, who she owed a lot to, quite a bit of trouble. Now that Mariel had power, there was no reason for her to hold back.

Even if it was the power of gods or demons…

"...So you're saying you came back with no results?"

"...Yes, Your Majesty."

The king was clearly in a bad mood. The emissary he had sent to that viscountess had finally returned, but with absolutely nothing to show for it. It was no wonder the king was displeased.

"I did go to the household of the viscountess... I had assumed she would easily be pressured into spilling secrets and signing a contract favorable to us if I gave her your name, Your Majesty, but Count Maslias, of her parent house, was in attendance, as well..."

"And you failed to get her to speak about the Goddess, her messenger, or anything else, and she refused to come to the capital out of respect for me or come under my patronage?"

"Indeed. Each time I brought up the matter, the count interjected that it would be cruel to have an underage child go to the capital now, after she had lost her family so recently and was still in distress from the incident with her uncle. He insisted this was an important time for her, as the new viscountess, and that she must focus on tending to her domain...

"And when I brought up bringing her under your patronage, he claimed that was his role as the head of her parent house. With Your Majesty being in the capital so far away, you would not be able to provide support in a timely manner if something were to happen to her...

"I thought that forcing her to attend the royal court against her will and that of her parent house, while she is already in another noble house's faction, could have caused a major issue..."

"And she had been told by the Goddess not to talk to anyone about her, so she refused to speak on the matter... But you must have learned something by threatening or bribing her servants. What did they tell you?"

Chapter 36: Trouble

"W-Well, Your Majesty, none of them agreed to speak a single word... I did hint at their own lives and their family's lives being in danger, but..."

"What happened?"

"They said to do as I pleased. Then they smiled an uncanny smile...

Their expressions told me that, if I did anything, I would incur the wrath of the Goddess and die for sure. There was such certainty in their faces..."

"..."

Come to think of it, there was no way they would betray anyone who was loved by the Goddess. And the goddess in question was the infamous Celestine. Although benevolent, she wasn't exactly meticulous and didn't care too much about the lives of individual humans. What disaster would result from betraying the human that this Goddess had taken a liking to...?

Not to mention, this was the wise, delicate, fourteen-year-old noble girl who was kind to commoners. It was hard to believe anyone would double-cross her.

...It appeared the plan had ended in failure. The king understood this well.

A young, unmarried, aristocrat girl who was blessed by the Goddess. No one was so foolish that they couldn't see her value. Naturally, her parent house and those of her faction would refuse to let her go.

He had to get her to come to the capital for a courtesy call so he could make an agreement with her directly, before the leader of her faction made a move. And he had to handle this all quite properly.

Although his authority was limited compared to other kingdoms, he was still a king. It wasn't impossible for him to use his influence as king to get a lower-class noble, and an underage girl at that, to make an agreement that was favorable to him. And once an official contract was made, it would be too late for her parent house or faction leader to do anything about it. After all, this would be an official agreement between the head of a noble house and the king.

However, his attempt to have his emissary contact her in private was blocked by the count, who was the head of her parent house. His efforts had ended in vain.

That sneaky approach wouldn't work anymore.

In fact, Count Maslias had already taught her all about this tactic, so it was unlikely that she would agree to such invitations or contracts.

He had no choice but to approach her as a good, kind king. And if he could foist one of his sons on her…

But using a good-looking young man as bait was an obvious tactic, used by aristocrats who had sons who were of age. If the viscountess came to the capital, he could…

The king's head hurt just thinking about it.

"Well, her faction leader may get a bit carried away, but the other factions should band together to keep him in check. At least, I hope so…"

It appeared there would be many ordeals to come for Mariel. Ordeals that Kaoru would be jealous of, if she were to hear about them…

Though, Kaoru had claimed that she would refuse any man who wanted her just for her position as the Angel or for her potions. So, perhaps Mariel wouldn't be shrieking with joy, but instead raising her voice for a legitimate cry for help.

And the day Mariel would have no choice but to go to the capital wasn't too far in the future…

Idle Chat: Celes Strawberries

"I'll be going to that person's place today. Ehe, ehehehe..." Celestine muttered to herself with a big grin on her face.

Today was another day in which she would report on Kaoru's status...or, rather, to go visit the manager of Earth.

"Ahhh, I am ever so grateful to Kaoru! Not only did she come up with the reason that I was able to meet him, but she gave me the great idea of checking in on the world regularly so we would have something in common and things to talk about! And all her antics give me plenty of exciting things to talk about. It's almost as if she's doing it on purpose...

"Ah! Maybe she really *is* doing it on purpose! Ohh, how wonderful you are, my only friend! I never knew how splendid it is to have friends!"

She was speaking much more candidly about "that person" than ever before. ...And although she referred to him as such, he wasn't technically a person. It seemed she was getting much closer to him, emotionally speaking.

In the meantime, her one-sided feeling of friendship toward Kaoru grew ever stronger.

Celestine's main body...the name of which was rather impossible for humans to pronounce...saw humans as something akin to how humans saw water fleas. But to the Celestine that was a mere sliver of her main body, which had her abilities lowered to make it possible for her to communicate with humans, she saw humans she took a liking to the same way humans saw chicks or hamsters.

However, she perceived most humans as akin to bugs, and humans she disliked were like mosquitoes or cockroaches to her. So, if any of them annoyed her or got in her way, she didn't hesitate to dispose of them.

Kaoru was somewhere around the level of a kitten she had received from someone she liked.

But her feelings of appreciation and friendship toward Kaoru were real and specific only to her.

"In any case, I need to seize this opportunity! I can't be losing to that old lady from the #§♭÷⊇ƒ£ dimension or anyone else!"

It appeared she had rivals, as well...

But it was a mystery how old they were if Celestine considered them to be old, while she had lived for millions of years herself...

But regardless of the life form's age, Celestine, That Person, the Old Lady, and all of her other rivals were nothing more than mere fractions of their main bodies, and since each of them had lowered their rates and levels of thinking so that they could communicate with the life forms of their respective worlds, they were all in a similar state.

...In other words, they did each vary to some degree, but they weren't all that different from Celestine.

The current Celestine had merely adopted an appearance similar to the creatures of her world, and she had no need to mimic the form of a human when visiting That Person, but That Person also happened to take the form of the same creatures, so she always visited him with this appearance, happy that they had matching looks.

"Okay, perfect! Here I go!" Celestine fixed up her appearance, and after checking herself several times, she teleported across dimensions.

As an aside, Celestine's breasts were small because, within the standards of her species, it wasn't considered beautiful to have unnecessary lumps of fat hanging off their bodies, having things that could inhibit movement attached to them, or having meaningless curves.

As a species that had no concept of sexual relations or raising children via breastfeeding, they considered small, compact, tight, and efficient bodies to be superior and therefore beautiful.

Celestine had actually made Kaoru's breasts slightly smaller than her original body's as a gesture of kindness when reconstructing her, and even made it so they wouldn't get any bigger through eating or exercise.

…It was done out of consideration. She thought it would make Kaoru happy…

It was completely unnecessary…

"H-How do you do…" Celestine opened with a greeting similar to that of a human's. It had only been the blink of an eye since they last met, by their standards, but it must have been far too long in Celestine's mind.

"Oh, hey, Celes. Thanks for stopping by all the time…"

"N-Not at all, I like reporting to you about Kaoru…" Celestine said shyly.

Since they didn't make use of the concepts of having lovers or getting married, nothing made them happier than having someone wonderful know about them, having another think favorably of them, or having others rely on them in an emergency and relying on them. Of course, this didn't apply to her main body but rather that of the lowest-grade offspring like this Celestine.

Therefore, Celestine was in the height of happiness at the moment.

Meanwhile, the other offspring, who were of a slightly higher level than Celestine, watched her through monitors in other dimensions, writhing at the sight.

Idle Chat: Celes Strawberries

"So bittersweet!!!" From the perspectives of the other offspring, it was like thirty-something-year-old older sisters watching their younger sister getting excited about her first love. They no longer felt such emotions themselves, but watching their younger sibling experience it made them feel strangely happy and entertained...

"Kaoru to the Eyes of the Goddess!"

"This is the Eyes of the Goddess."

The intonation was a bit off, so "Kaoru" sounded more like "Kirk." This was just a matter of Kaoru's preferences. She had taken a tool out of the Item Box to contact the children of the Eyes of the Goddess. The tool in question was the "sound resonance crystal set," which contained a potion inside of it. It came in a set, as the name suggested, and when you spoke into one of them, the sound resonated through the other crystal to relay the message.

...Though, officially, it was just a potion container that came with such functions.

Kaoru had to open the Item Box and check it to notice any calls from the kids, but the children answered right away whenever she called from her end. To them, the idea of leaving the house that Kaoru had left them unattended, or not having someone on watch with the sound resonance crystal set — their only means of communication with Kaoru — was inconceivable.

So, Kaoru had contacted them regularly, once every few days, to make sure there were no issues at the orphanage or in the royal capital. She kind of had to because, otherwise, the worried orphans would have constantly tried to get hold of her, and she would have been bombarded with alerts every time she opened the Item Box.

"Anything new?"

"Nothing in particular. Oh, Achille just went through his ceremony to officially become a baron. Then he brought up the idea of Lolotte becoming his lover, and there was a big argument with everyone else at the workshop."

"Ah…"

Achille, the third son of Baron Lyodart's household and one of the workers at the Maillart Workshop, was to receive the title of baron for his contributions in the plan to keep the Goddess in the country. The reason for him receiving his title was supposedly because he had assisted the Goddess and worked as a driving force in welcoming her to their country.

In truth, they had wanted to make Kaoru royalty or at least a high-ranking aristocrat, but they figured she wouldn't care about ranks made up by humans. So, in order to increase what little chance they had, they decided to put men of marriageable age associated with her into circumstances that would make it easier for her to marry them.

Hector, of Earl Adan's household, was already the firstborn son in the family, so he was fine as-is.

Achille had been making moves on Lolotte, the girl from the Eyes of the Goddess who had been named Kaoru's successor for handling the domestic duties at the Maillart Workshop, but a baron couldn't just take an orphan girl as a wife, so the idea of being his mistress had been brought up.

"The guys at the workshop wouldn't have said anything about the third-born son of a low-ranking aristocrat with no title prospects. Making her his mistress would have been one thing, but they couldn't stay silent when he proposed to make her his lover without any official standing, which would have meant their child wouldn't have inherited his status or rights as a noble."

A mistress was similar to a concubine. Their arrangement would be officially acknowledged by the lawful wife, the man would take care of her expenses, and their child would inherit the aristocrat's status and rights, unlike a lover, who would never be officially recognized.

But for an orphan, even that would be like a Cinderella story. And a commoner was really in no position to argue with a baron. But to the others at the workshop, he was still Achille, their colleague, despite his noble position. And they all felt the need to protect their friend, Lolotte.

"Well, then I guess it's really up to what she wants... Why don't you let her decide?"

"We will. Oh, and Achille's older brother's wife came to check on us. She said she was worried now that you weren't around to take care of us. But when we told her that all you did was lie around and that you didn't cook, clean, or do laundry much, so we always took care of ourselves, she went home looking really mad."

"Gya..."

"Gya?"

"Gyaaaaaa!!!"

Kaoru then had Emile and Belle take over the conversation and curled up with her head clutched in her hands...

Chapter 37: My First Errand

"Kaoru, I want to go outside."

"Hm? Sure. The morning shift's almost over, so wait just a little longer, okay? So, where are we going?"

Layette was sitting on Kaoru's lap as usual when she brought it up, and Kaoru had replied assuming she would go with her. Of course, there was no other possible option.

But...

"Actually, I want to go by myself."

"Wh-Whaaaaaat?!"

Kaoru was flabbergasted.

D-D-Does she hate me now? She never wanted to leave my side before... Is this her rebellious phase? Or maybe she's becoming independent? Ohh, what do I do...

Kaoru was completely losing it.

Chapter 37: My First Errand

But Layette had been sold by her parents and kidnapped, and the gate guards had all been part of the ploy. No one could blame her if she didn't trust adults.

"Wh-Wh-Wh-" *What should I do?!* "Wh-Wh-Wh-" *Where are you going?!* "Wh-Wh-Wh-" *Who put her up to thiiiiiis?!*

"I have no idea what you're trying to say…"

Kaoru was shot down by Layette's calm response…

"…So that's why."

"…"

After Kaoru had questioned Layette in a panic, she had gone on to explain…

She was now six years old and would be seven very soon, but she was always with Kaoru, who protected her and took care of her every need. She did nothing on her own, and hadn't made any progress in any meaningful way. She had come to think the situation had to change for her own good.

"L-Layette… That's so respectable of you…" Kaoru couldn't help but hug Layette tightly.

"…This is what I mean!"

"Whaaat… But you're supposed to provide emotional support…"

"No, I want to be useful to you, Kaoru!"

"I mean, you're very useful for emotional support…"

"Nooo! Not like thaaat!!!" Layette bopped Kaoru on her flat chest with closed fists, hopped off of her lap, then ran up the stairs to the second floor.

"What…? Whaaat… Whaaaaaaaaat?!"

Speechless. Kaoru was completely speechless. As she sat there in a shocked stupor, Francette watched her with a look of pity.

"So you think I might be a little overprotective?"

"Not that you 'might' be, you absolutely *are* overprotective of her!"

"Whaaat...?" Kaoru was taken aback by Francette's unusually firm attitude.

"Think of it this way. If there was someone you really cared about and you wanted to do things for them and make them happy, but all they did was fawn over you without letting you do anything, how would you feel? Would it be fun wasting your time away getting spoiled without really doing anything when you wanted to be useful to them?"

"Ah..."

Francette was right. At six or seven in Japan, Layette would have been in elementary school. Elementary school was where everyone studied, played with friends, got in fights, went on adventures, and experienced all sorts of things to undergo great physical and mental growth.

Meanwhile, Layette spent the vast majority of her day sitting on Kaoru's lap under her constant protection. It was incredible that Layette had come to realize on her own that something had to change when she was living an easy, happy, and stable life...

Chapter 37: My First Errand

"I'm so proud of Layette!" Kaoru was so happy that she couldn't help but beam in ecstasy.

"This is what I'm talking about!!!" It seemed Francette was getting seriously ticked off. And she was talking to a so-called goddess...

"...So you're telling me to push Layette away?"

"I wouldn't go that far, but..."

Now that Kaoru had calmed down, Francette began to talk about how to remedy the issue.

"In any case, if you wish for Layette to live a fulfilling life without hurting her or hampering her personal growth, you cannot go on as things are now. You will need to respect her independence more, let her think on her own, and get her used to being alone... Otherwise, without you...no, even *with* you around, she won't be able to do anything on her own. Is that how you want her to turn out?"

"Urgh..." Her knowledge about NEETs, shut-ins, and the prevalence of communication issues from her previous life made her realize she could ruin Layette's life, and Kaoru began to sweat.

"Wh-What should I do...?" Kaoru asked in a fluster, and Francette replied decisively,

"You must let her do things on her own! Like going outside!"

"That's exactly what she said in the first place!!!"

...And so, Layette was given the permission to go out on her own.

"Okay, I'm going now!"

"Be careful! Don't eat anything you find on the ground! Don't follow any strangers who talk to you! Don't go into back alleys, even if a boy asks you..."

"Cut it out, Kaoru!"

Kaoru stood frozen in shock, and Layette ran off outside.

Kaoru quickly recomposed herself and gave the order in a hushed tone. "Francette, I'm counting on you!"

"Yes, please leave it to me!" With that, Francette ran off after Layette.

After the earlier conversation, Kaoru had a conversation with Francette, Roland, Emile, and Belle, and decided to send Layette out on a warrior's journey. ...Though she would be back later that day, of course.

It wasn't just Francette — Emile and Belle also got requests from Kaoru sometimes. From everyone else's perspective, this was a divine edict, a heaven-sent opportunity for them to be of use to Kaoru. Layette was the only one who didn't see it that way, and she was beginning to feel like a useless good-for-nothing. "I'd be just like Old Roland if I stayed like this," she had said, and Roland was severely depressed when he heard about it.

In any case, Kaoru had to give Layette some work and motivate her. Moreover, she wanted to take this opportunity to get her to interact with other children, play, exercise, and make her more social, so as to kill two birds with one stone. So the order Kaoru had given Layette was…

Chapter 37: My First Errand

"Infiltrate the orphanage and investigate whether the children there are worthy of the Goddess's blessing." ...In other words, it was an order for her to go mingle with them.

It was the first task Kaoru had tasked Layette within her capacity as the messenger of the Goddess. It was Layette's very first official errand. So, of course, Kaoru had to have someone support her from the shadows.

She'd already had Emile and Belle research the orphan group in question beforehand to make sure there weren't any thugs or child traffickers in the area scoping them out. Plus, they had found that their leader was a responsible kid who only permitted the minimum amount of crime that was absolutely necessary for survival. He was also diligent and took measures to ensure any damage done to the victims would be minimal while avoiding unnecessary violence or exploitation.

If Layette ended up becoming friends with them and it was determined that they weren't worthy of the Goddess's blessing, it would have made Layette sad. That was why Kaoru made sure she would be going to a group that would pass the test.

Francette gave Kaoru an exasperated look when she heard this, but decided not to say anything. Though, it was unclear whether that was out of kindness, or if Francette had just given up on her...

It was extremely rare for Layette to say with such a serious tone that she absolutely didn't want Kaoru to follow her, so she had no choice but to peek out and watch Layette from behind a tree, whispering, "Layette..." like she was Hyuma's older sister.

Kaoru didn't want to ignore Layette's request or break any promises...or rather, she was more worried about hurting her when she found out, or Layette ending up hating her, so she couldn't take any risks, no matter how small. And so, Kaoru had given up on following Layette in secret.

But Layette had only told Kaoru not to follow her. ...Indeed, she never said someone else couldn't do so. That was why Kaoru had sent Francette. Kaoru had actually wanted to send Emile and Belle, as well, but Francette strongly disagreed, since that course of action would result in leaving Kaoru alone. And since Roland had no training in guarding someone while hiding, he would only get in the way. She really didn't seem to think about Roland at all...

"Th-There it is..." Layette had arrived at some grassy plains by a riverbed. A small distance from the river's surface, there was something like a little shanty built out of scrap wood and long pieces of grass...in fact, it could just barely be called a shelter for rain. Around it, there were five or six children who seemed to range from four to five years old and seven to eight years old.

Apparently, they were outside because it was better than being crammed in that stuffy "rain shelter." They were all too young to be living on their own. The older ones were likely out earning money or gathering food, and the somewhat-older seven- to eight-year-olds were watching over the younger kids.

This place was close to the sea, and due to the layout of the terrain, the river water wouldn't reach it. It didn't rain much, either. Even if the water level did rise, they probably wouldn't have a problem abandoning their dingy sleeping spot, and they could easily rebuild another with the pieces of wood that would wash up with the tide.

The convenience of the location just by the riverbed outweighed the possibility of the water rising to a dangerous level, so it was hard to give it up. To anyone who didn't have access to the communal well, having moving water for drinking, laundry, bathing, and defecation was extremely important. The river supported their life in many respects.

"Okay, time to get to work!" With that, Layette began walking over to the other children.

The children stared at Layette with looks of suspicion.

Layette stopped several meters away, then said to them, "I-Is business boomin'?"

"What the heck was thaaat?!"

Just what was Kaoru teaching Layette…?

"…So, you tryin' to tell us you're an orphan, too? Even though you're so clean and wearing fancy clothes?" The boy who seemed to be the oldest of the group stared at Layette dubiously, but she seemed unfazed.

Indeed, Layette was feeling fearless right now. After all, she was carrying out a top-secret mission for the Goddess, so there was no need to worry about her own life.

"Yup! My parents sold me, then I was kidnapped on the way to being taken to the traffickers! I was about to be a slave, or a sacrifice, or a 'plaything,' but I was saved instead!"

Bfff! The kids all spit at once. Even the ones who didn't know what a 'plaything' was understood the concept of being sold, as well as what traffickers, kidnapping, and slaves were. These were all dangers that could threaten them at any time, so the older kids had warned them repeatedly.

And it would have been one thing if her parents had just died, but that they had sold her was almost too heavy to consider. They thought they were in a bad spot, but there were always those who were worse off. They didn't know whether to be happy or sad about that…

In any case, the children understood well that this girl was an orphan like them.

"I'm traveling around with the person who saved me and we're staying in the city for now. She told me there were kids at this riverbank, so I should come by for a while..."

"..."

Whoever her caretaker was, she must have seen their shelter if she knew about the children here. Naturally, she would know that they were a group of orphans and barely had anything to eat... Considering she had sent her here anyway...

...Had she been abandoned?

Layette had learned many things from Kaoru. One of them being the concept of lying.

According to Kaoru...

"You can lie when you need to, but you shouldn't lie when it's not necessary."

"If you're not lying but just so happen to forget to include a piece of information, it's not your fault if someone gets the wrong idea. That's their own fault for making assumptions."

"It's okay to tell lies that make people laugh or make them happy."

"For every lie you tell, furnish it with ninety-nine truths."

"If you want someone to believe you, you need to believe in your own lie first."

Such were the lessons for gifted children that were imparted to Layette, though it may have been a bit early to teach them to a six-year-old.

"U-Uh, I-I see. W-W-Well, make yourself at home..."

"Hm? O-Okay..."

Chapter 37: My First Errand

Layette was rather confused by the boy's sudden shift to an awkwardly kind demeanor.

"W-Wanna play with us?" The invitation came from a girl who was about the same age as the boy who had just spoken.

"Yeah!" This was Layette's first interaction with children around her age since leaving her village. She felt honored, relieved, and happy whenever she was with Kaoru, but it was far from a true friendship. Children needed other children...

"...It appears Layette has succeeded in infiltrating their ranks." Francette sat on the branch of a thick tree, watching the orphans from a distance. Since there was nothing obstructing the view from the riverbed, she had to stay somewhat distant or risk being seen. She was able to check on Layette's safety, but she wasn't able to hear what they were talking about.

"Well, a baby's job is to sleep and cry, and a child's job is to play. As for knights..." With that, Francette gripped the hilt of her sword lightly. "Our job is to defeat our enemies and fulfill our duty. No matter how simple...or impossible...that may be. I must carry out orders from the one I've sworn loyalty to!"

"...Hm? Who's that kid?" The five children who returned seemed to range from around ten years old to thirteen or fourteen years old. There were three boys and two girls.

"Fancy clothes she's wearing... Why is a girl like her here? Sherry! What if someone thinks we kidnapped her? We'll all be arrested and enslaved! Why didn't you stop this? Who brought her?!" the oldest boy, who seemed to be the leader of the group, shouted angrily, but the girl named Sherry, who had been left behind, shook her head.

"...She came here on her own. She's one of us."

"What...?" The leader boy didn't seem to believe it, but Sherry should have understood such dangers. And although this newcomer's clothes and clean-looking face and hands did stand out a bit, the rest of her did blend in with the others. She wasn't looking down on the others, either, but seemed to regard them as equals.

"...But even if she wants to stay, it'll all be over if her parents come looking for her. Even if she was abused, her parents would be ashamed to have her be seen with us. They could even blame us and say we kidnapped her..."

"She said she has no parents, and the person who takes care of her told her to come here."

"..." The leader boy listened to Sherry and thought that this person who took care of this newcomer girl must have been keeping her clean only because it would be a nuisance if she began attracting fleas and lice. It was only natural for him to think so.

"I see... Well, I'm Maloi. I'm the leader around here. Anyway, come visit anytime you want!" the boy said after thinking about it for a brief moment. It seemed he had accepted Layette into the group.

After spending some time with the orphans, Layette saw that the older children were beginning to prepare a meal and decided to take her leave.

"I'm gonna go home for today. Thanks for playing with me!" Layette said to the others and trotted off.

She had realized that if she stayed any longer, the other children would try to share what little food they had with her, and she didn't want to put them in that situation.

...Or perhaps she simply preferred Kaoru's cooking over their not-so-tasty and meager food...

Chapter 37: My First Errand

In any case, Sherry had thought Layette had nowhere left to go home to. Layette casually strolled away, leaving the bewildered Sherry asking, "Huh? What?"

"...So that's what happened. Juta, Rosche, and Sherry were all so nice!"

"Mhm, great job, Layette! Keep up the good work tomorrow, okay?"

"Yeah!"

"...How was it, Francette?"

"She seemed to be enjoying her time with the other orphans. There was nothing out of the ordinary, and as Emile had already found out during his preliminary investigation, they all seemed to be sincere and decent, despite their circumstances."

"Thanks. Let's make tomorrow her last day of the mission, then. If Layette wants to visit them on her own afterward, that's up to her. She's free to go there if she wants, instead of going there because I ordered her to..."

"Yes..." There was a gentle look in Francette's eyes, as well. Francette wasn't hated, exactly, but because of her serious, inflexible, and stubborn personality, she didn't have many friends she could open up to and have a heart-to-heart conversation with. It wasn't as if she had scary eyes...

The next night, Kaoru told Layette, "Those kids pass. Now I know they're worthy of receiving help if something happens to them, so your investigation is done."

There was a tinge of sadness to Layette's expression, and Kaoru added, "So you can go play with them whenever you want." Layette was delighted.

Afterward, Layette went to visit the orphans from time to time.

...Of course, Francette or Emile secretly watched over her when she did. There was no way the super-protective Kaoru would let her walk around outside by herself.

"Cops and Robbers is when you split up between guards and robbers and try to catch the other team or run away!"

"The Daruma Doll Fell Over is when one person is 'it,' and the others..."

...And so, Layette taught the orphans the games she had learned from Kaoru.

Overprotective as always, Kaoru had taught Layette all sorts of games from Japan so she could blend in with the other children more easily. Kaoru had also made sure to teach Layette games that wouldn't require any additional gear. There was no chair to play Fruit Basket, and they had no can to play Kick the Can.

"What's a daruma?"

"Umm... Someone without arms or legs, I think."

Chapter 37: My First Errand

"Hey, you wanna play by making some person without arms or legs fall over?! That's not humane! Oh, I guess that's why one person is called 'it'..."

...That wasn't it at all.

In any case, the simple, yet refined games from Japan were a huge hit among the orphans. And since there were too few members of the group that stayed home, they usually played once the older kids came back, or asked kids over from other orphan groups. It didn't take long for the games to spread among orphans from all over the city.

Layette began solidifying her position among the orphans as someone who came up with fun games.

It was Francette's turn to be on watch duty today. Francette sat on a tree branch that had become her regular resting spot. Emile had been using the same spot as well, and they had each modified it for their own comfort, like adding a little hook to hang a canteen or shaving a bit of the branch to make it easier to sit on.

...It was just like how children liked to make "secret bases."

Once the season changed and the leaves fell off, they would have to find another spot to observe from. A good spot that wasn't exposed to the cold wind...

"Urgh... Oh no, my stomach..." Francette was a knight. As such, whenever she had to eat or go to the restroom while on duty at her previous job, she'd had someone else cover for her. She wasn't the only one on duty then, and it was normal for someone to be available to swap in at any time.

It wasn't as if she was a ninja who had been trained not to eat or go to the restroom while on duty. Not eating was one thing, but hydrating and…relieving herself…was necessary. And she had done so on this mission several times already.

"There isn't much to obstruct the view or hide behind out at the riverbed…" Francette muttered to herself as she made her way toward a spot some distance away.

Although her real age was in her late thirties, and it wasn't as if she hadn't done it many times before, she did have reservations about doing her business where there was a possibility of someone seeing her. Especially when it was 'number two'…

But by then, Francette was no longer worried at all about the orphans, and she figured it would be fine to take her eyes off Layette for ten minutes or so. Kaoru was just abnormally overprotective, she told herself.

Indeed, it was the same thought process as those who inevitably came to regret their foolish carelessness later on…

"There she is!" Two adults approached Layette as she played with the children in the stay-at-home group, and began sprinting after yelling as much.

"Begin attack!" Sherry, the leader of today's stay-at-home group, shouted without hesitation, and the orphans immediately stopped what they were doing, ducked, and gripped an appropriately-sized rock in each hand. They launched the rocks in their right hands toward the adults, then passed the rocks in their left hands to their right, and followed up with another toss.

Duck, pick up rocks, throw twice, duck again.

The six orphans besides Layette threw rock after rock as if they had trained for it many times…in fact, they certainly must have. Since they were at the riverbed, they had plenty of rocks to reload with.

Chapter 37: My First Errand

Kidnappers who would take children to turn into illegal slaves or playthings... Men who killed children just for fun... The orphans must have trained countless times to protect themselves from such fiends. For children that were only four to eight years old, their attacks were highly coordinated.

Kids their age had no chance of outrunning adults. Kidnappers could easily catch any one of them and take them away. That was why they had put their all into throwing rocks, the one method with which even children could stand up to adults, as long as they landed a solid hit.

It wasn't as if the number of captured kids would increase if they failed. One adult would only be able to take one child with them at a time, and it would be exceedingly difficult for them to subdue two at once. In addition, if they wanted to be inconspicuous with their kidnapping, one child between two adults was probably their limit.

"Damned brats!" The thrown rocks hit the adults many times, but with their arms protecting their heads and the attacks landing on their limbs and body through their clothes, the children weren't strong enough to break any bones or knock them unconscious. ... Though it was enough to cause plenty of pain.

There wasn't much distance between them, so the sprinting adults quickly reached the children and began punching and kicking at full force, neutralizing them immediately.

It wasn't enough to kill anyone, but the attacks were brutal enough on their young bodies that they could have ended up with broken bones or permanent damage. Even if captured like this, their value would be greatly lowered. They were far too thoughtless for kidnappers.

Since Layette didn't participate in the rock-throwing, she simply stood there flabbergasted, without receiving any of the violence.

"All right, we took care of the pests. Now, let's get our prey!"

At this point, Layette finally realized something. The adults weren't after the orphans. They were after her. She was certainly the best dressed and cleanest of the group, and would likely fetch a high price. Therefore, they would focus on securing Layette, the target that would yield them the highest return.

That was why they didn't care if they injured or even killed the other children. It explained why they had punched and kicked them with full force. They had used excessive violence as retaliation for the pain from the rocks that were thrown at them.

"Grrr…" Layette bared her teeth.

The set of teeth that had caused some serious damage when she had chomped down on Francette's neck…

Wsh! They grabbed on to each of Layette's shoulders from both sides and tried to lift her up.

Just then, her neck twisted around and…

Chomp.

"Gyaaaaaa!!!" The man hadn't raised his voice even when taking a direct hit from a rock, but it seemed he couldn't bear this pain.

Layette was only six years old, but she had pretty powerful jaws. And her teeth were tiny.

If their diameter were half that of an adult's, the surface area would be one fourth the size. …In other words, they were extremely sharp. And they were backed by the full force of Layette's bite.

Not to mention, her upper canines were very developed. The difference in power between getting stomped with flat heels and with high heels had already been demonstrated on Francette's neck.

CHAPTER 37: MY FIRST ERRAND

"How is your neck's range of mobility so wide?! What are you, a wolf?!" the man who hadn't gotten bitten said, but the one who had didn't have any patience for such observations.

"Ahhh! Sh-She's gonna rip a chunk outta me! Get off me, damn iiit!!!" But pushing her away or pulling on her head would only add leverage for her to tear off a piece of his arm meat. And so, he changed his tactics and started punching her instead.

"Hey! We're not supposed to hurt that one!"

"Shut up! Who's gonna pay if I follow that order and lose an arm, huh?! Are you? Are you gonna give me a thousand gold coins and take care of me forever?!" There was nothing that could be said in response to that. It was true that the chances of her taking out a piece of his arm and rendering it useless weren't zero. But he didn't want to take personal responsibility for that if it happened, so he could only shrug his shoulders and watch. He was just glad it wasn't him that had been bitten...

Layette refused to release his arm, even as he punched her in the face and stomach. Flustered, the man drew his dagger with his left hand in a flash of rage.

"H-Hey, don't..." The other man quickly moved to stop him, but the man with the dagger raised his weapon.

He intended to strike her with the hilt rather than the blade, but a blow with full force behind it would easily break such a young child's bones, whether her ribcage or her skull.

Down came his left hand, and...it swung at empty air.

"...Huh? What? Wha..." He had missed the girl's body completely. Confused, he checked his left arm and immediately realized why.

Chapter 37: My First Errand

His arm had been completely severed from the elbow, with nothing extending beyond it. It was no wonder his swing had missed.

…Yes, he understood now. It made total sense.

"Gyaaaaaaaaagh!!!"

"…What are you doing?" The man realized something was off and shook off Layette as she released her hold, then he cried out and clutched his left elbow.

The other man leapt back in a panic and drew his dagger.

There she stood, the blade in her hand spotless as it vibrated at supersonic speed, splattering specks of blood all around it. A young girl…or, at least, she looked like one.

"…Just what…do you think you're doing…?" She was a young girl clad in knightly armor, smiling pleasantly. But her smile didn't reach her eyes. While her mouth formed a smile, a different emotion emanated from her entire body. It was…

Rage. Hatred. And again, rage.

Rage for the injury they had caused to her comrade, who also served the Goddess.

Rage for injuring such an innocent little girl.

Regret and self-hatred for letting this happen due to her own foolishness…and rage.

Fear and rage at herself for betraying the Goddess's trust, failing to fulfill her divine duty.

Rage, rage, rage, rage, rage…

Wham! …Crack.

The man's dagger didn't even have a chance to touch her before her blade sank deep into his side. His ribs broke, their shards digging directly into his organs. He fell facedown, unable to speak, only making wheezing noises as he struggled to breathe.

Francette ignored the downed man, walked over to the other man who was gripping his arm that was severed at the elbow, and kicked him down. Then...

Crack! Thud! Crack!

She broke both of his knees and his right arm.

"Gyaaaaaa!!!" The fallen men not only couldn't get up, but they couldn't even back away. Seeing this, Francette produced what seemed to be a metallic test tube.

"Layette! It's Lady Kaoru's potion. Drink it!" But Layette shook her head in refusal.

"Give it to the others! I'll be okay!" From Francette's view, her first priority was to protect Layette, her second priority was to protect Layette, and her third priority was to protect Layette. She would only bother to help some orphans she didn't know if she had time to spare.

Despite her current appearance, Francette was in the latter half of her thirties and had a rather dry and intense personality... Or perhaps she was just faithful to her orders as a knight and servant of the Goddess. As long as it didn't affect her mission, she would even help strangers in need. ...Probably.

But for now, she had to prioritize her number one objective, which was to protect and treat Layette.

...And yet, Layette herself wanted her friends to be helped instead of her, and upon careful inspection, she didn't look too bad. Her breathing was stable, and she was able to communicate normally. Those were signs that she wasn't suffering from any serious injuries like internal ruptures or broken bones digging into vital organs or thick veins, so she likely wasn't in any immediate danger.

And some of the children who had been punched and kicked still lay there completely motionless. The possibility of ruptured organs and permanent injuries couldn't be denied.

Chapter 37: My First Errand

Not to mention, if something were to happen to them, Layette would blame herself and carry that trauma for the rest of her life. Francette didn't just need to protect Layette's physical body, but also her heart. It was only natural.

And so, she stuck her fingers in her mouth and made a loud whistling noise toward a different tree than the one she had been hiding in.

Piiiiiiiiiii!

A crow that had been resting on the tree's branch flew over, circling above Francette's head. Francette signaled an "X" with both arms, then the crow fled off toward the center of the city. The crow was a messenger that Kaoru had left with Francette, just in case something happened, and she had taught it about three simple signals.

Once Francette confirmed that the crow had flown off, she nodded toward Layette. Despite the pain from the punch she had to the face, and the fatigue in her jaw and teeth from biting as hard as she could, she tried not to let it show and forced an awkward smile.

Francette pretended not to notice her strained effort and turned away from Layette, walking toward the other children. She woke an unconscious boy, forced his mouth open with her finger, popped open the metallic container, and poured its contents into the boy's mouth. Francette then moved on to another heavily injured yet still-conscious girl, opened another potion container, and gently pressed it against her mouth.

"This is medicine. Drink it!" Despite her confusion, the young girl seemed to realize Francette wasn't an enemy and drank it down as ordered.

"...It doesn't hurt..."

"H-How...?"

The kids that had taken the potions sat there with blank looks on their faces, unable to process what was happening.

There were four more children splayed out at the riverbed, but Kaoru had only supplied Francette with two emergency potions. There was nothing else she could do.

"Luce, get some wood for splints and something to tie them! I'll go get water!"

"Got it! I need you to find some herbs that can stop the bleeding around the river too!"

"On it!" The two kids had regained their senses and sped off into action.

…It seemed the orphan kids were far more useful than Francette…

"So… What happened…?"

"Um, well, you see…"

"Whaaat haaappened heeere…?" Kaoru had come running at full speed after getting the emergency message and a call for her to mobilize. And…

She was scary. Kaoru was terrifying. Especially the look in her eyes…

"What did I tell you, Franceeette…?"

"U-Um, I, I'm so sorry!!!" Francette said, apologizing desperately.

Although she couldn't help nature calling and it was only for a few minutes, it was her fault for taking her eyes away from the person she was supposed to be protecting and moving to a spot where she couldn't react right away.

A big part of the fault lay with Kaoru for not considering this situation and therefore not preparing someone to switch with her in shifts, but Francette wasn't someone who could shift blame onto other people, especially not to a goddess. So, Kaoru continued to

Chapter 37: My First Errand

berate her, becoming enraged as soon as she saw the scene of the incident.

"Kaoru! Hurry and give Layette a potion!"

"Ah!"

It should have been the obvious course of action, but it didn't even cross Kaoru's mind until Emile's reminder. It seemed that she had completely lost her cool.

"Layette, drink this!"

There were still four orphans who were injured, but now that Kaoru was here, the number of potions wasn't an issue. If Layette started arguing about getting to the others first, it would only waste more time. She correctly surmised this from Kaoru's personality and the current situation, and drank the potion she was handed without argument.

"Thank goodness... So, why did...?"

"Before we talk, the others need potions, too!"

"Huh? O-Okay, got it!"

As soon as Kaoru saw Layette on the ground with swollen cheeks and tears on her face, she couldn't see anything else in her field of view. Not even the other orphans, the sack of meat struggling to breathe, or the worm crawling on the ground...

"So, what happened here?" Kaoru asked in a low voice. She had given potions to each of the orphans and sat before the dumbstruck children, as well as the meat sack and worm still on the ground, trying to prevent her rage from showing in her face.

Sh-She's so scary...

Francette and Layette had explained the situation to Kaoru, and she had decided to hear from the worm next. That is, the man whose left hand had been sliced off, followed by the rest of his limbs. The meat sack was in no state to talk...

"So, who put you up to this, what were you doing, and why?"

"..."

His face was contorted with pain and fear, but it seemed he had no intention of talking just because a little girl tried to intimidate him.

"I see..." Kaoru reached into her chest pocket and produced some salt. She held it in her hand, pulled out her hand from her pocket, then...

"There!" She threw it at the man's exposed wound on his left arm.

"Gyaaaaaaaaagh!!!"

Eeek!!! Francette, Layette, and the orphans shuddered at the fiendish act.

Emile and Belle were unfazed. To them, anything Kaoru did was justice. Whatever she did was undeniable. Not to mention, they were quietly angry about the orphans getting beaten half to death, as well as Layette getting hurt, since they saw her as their beloved little sister. To them, orphans younger than them were all like their younger siblings.

Kaoru picked up the man's left arm from the ground.

"You know, I could still use my potions to put this arm back on. The cut was pretty clean, after all. But if the surface of the cut gets ruined..." With that, she picked up the dagger that was next to the arm and twisted it into the surface of the cut.

"S-Stop, nooooooooo!!!" She then peeled the nails off and gave it a couple quick stabs...

"S-Stop, no, stoppp!" No matter how much she damaged the severed arm, there was no way he could actually feel the pain. So why was he panicking so much?

Chapter 37: My First Errand

...There was no one there thinking that. The color had drained from the orphans' faces, and they were all shuddering in fear or hunched over and vomiting.

"Ahh... Might not be able to reattach this with it being so cut up like this..."

As she continued to dig at it with the dagger...

"W-Wait, stop! Please, fix it, reattach my armmm!"

Kaoru continued without even responding...

"I'll talk! I'll tell you anything! Reattach my arm, pleeease!!!"

"...So, someone hired you in the capital and told you to kidnap Layette because she could be used against me to follow orders and was the easiest to capture out of those close to me, her food costs wouldn't be too high, and she'd be easy to sell off once you were done with her?"

"Y-Yes!" the man replied earnestly, his arm having been reattached to his body. However, it hadn't immediately healed back to its original state. They had only used a lesser potion that healed it gradually and then secured it with a splint and bandages. It would properly reattach itself if he maintained this position, but one wrong move and it could fall right off again.

"Hm, I see..." she said in a flat, emotionless tone.

Hearing this, the orphans thought they were right in assuming Kaoru and the others didn't care about Layette.

"Hmm, I seeeee..."

Shiver...

"Hmmmmm, I...seeeeeeeee..."

"Gyaaaaaaaaa!!!"

The children instantly broke down in tears upon seeing Kaoru's face. Some of them peed their pants. The two would-be kidnappers had gone pale, their faces contorted in shock.

The man with the broken ribs had his organ damage healed with a healing potion as well, but the ribs themselves were still left as-is. A simple punch there could force the ribs back into his organs, so he couldn't even put up a fight against children.

Kaoru had explained to him that the potion was just a powerful painkiller and that his organs had been fine in the first place, but he should be able to tell that his own ribs were broken.

"Let's talk a little more about that, then, shall we...?"

Nod, nod, nod, nod...

A skilled swordswoman wielding absolute power. A merciless young girl with an inexplicably intimidating aura. And a boy and girl who seemed to be young hunters that didn't even twitch at her brutality, a look of fanaticism in their eyes. Not to mention the group of orphans who wouldn't hesitate to kill them with the wood scraps and rocks they gripped in their hands.

One wrong move and they'd be dead.

Attempted murder and kidnapping...

With so many witnesses, their corpses could be turned in to the guards for a handsome reward, and they wouldn't even be questioned. There was no reason for these people to show them any mercy. The only potential reward in keeping them alive was that it would save them the trouble of carrying their corpses, and they could get a bit of extra coin for selling them as judicial slaves.

Even then, there was always the possibility that they would prioritize the safety of the orphans and choose to beat the two of them to death as an example to any who might try something similar. They had to surrender completely, show remorse, and hope for mercy. That was the only way for these two to be saved...or rather, for them to survive.

Chapter 37: My First Errand

"So we still don't know who's behind all this…"

After continuing to question the two men for some time, we handed them over to the authorities. We were told we would get our share of the reward and profits from selling them as judicial slaves at a later date.

Of course, that money was to be spent on the orphans. Handing such a sum to them would all but guarantee they'd be robbed by thugs or other orphans, so we had to figure out a good solution, but…

Since I had told Belle to call for Roland during the questioning, the conversation with the officer went smoothly. The only value that Roland's existence had was that he made it easier to have discussions with external parties. He had to show his usefulness here, or there would be no point in providing for him.

Since Francette was away on her own duties (protecting Layette), Roland had left Emile and Belle to guard me and went wandering off by himself. He complained about missing his moment to shine, but it was his own fault for not being there. Why was he complaining to me?! And even if he did rush to them with me, his time to shine would have been long gone.

In any case, he was obviously a rich aristocrat no matter how you looked at him, and he did have the appearance of a somewhat capable swordsman. Having him around made a huge difference when making a report, compared to a bunch of underage children and young adults doing it by themselves.

It was best to make use of anything of convenience.

And so, we finished taking care of the orphans and handing over the criminals and went home to Convenience Store Belle…

"Well, I suppose whoever employed them would have no reason to tell them everything…"

Francette was right; the one pulling the strings wouldn't do such a thing. But it was likely some throwaway criminal who was hired by someone from the royal palace, an aristocrat, or one of the merchants who still suspected me or hadn't heard the new information about my hair and eye color. They wanted to connect with me to make a request or threaten me. They would use my abilities, name value, and connection with Celes to rise through the ranks.

...That was fine. That in itself was no problem.

Whether they were clever enough not to be fooled by the false information, didn't even have access to said information, or just wanted to take advantage of me, they were probably desperately working to provide for their own subordinates, dependents, and domain. That was fine.

...But the ones who intended to hurt Layette? They're done for.

"...I'll crush them."

"Yes?" Francette asked, her voice squeaking.

Emile and Belle nodded wordlessly, and Roland only shrugged lightly.

Those were their usual reactions. Indeed, it was just like usual...

Evening of that day, a maid came to shop at Convenience Store Belle and went home. Upon paying, she left a silver coin and a small piece of paper.

"You have a summons from an aristocrat in the royal capital. Declining is not an option, as this is coming from the leader of a faction under Count Maslias of your parent house. You are to meet him to discuss some matters that will be explained to you."

"...Perfect timing. Let's do this, then..."

Grin...

Chapter 38:
To the Capital

"Take care of the house in my absence, then."

"Yes, of course. Please return safely, my lady."

Mariel was now the head of the house rather than just the daughter of the viscount, but it seemed the servants still addressed her as they always had.

Well, I guess she was too young to be called madam or mistress. And the servants had likely worked under her for many years, so their relationship likely wouldn't change until she got married. They might even see her as the same young lady even after she got married. It would probably take some time until that habit died out...

Mariel was under the protection of Count Maslias, the head of her parent house...which meant that House Raphael as a whole was part of his faction, as well. In any case, a marquis and faction leader had sent what was basically an order to appear in the form of an invitation, so we decided to head to the capital.

Count Maslias had departed ahead of us to make some arrangements beforehand.

And why was I here now, you might ask...

"Time to go, Kaoru."

"Yes, my lady!"

That's the deal. After Mariel had contacted me, we had exchanged several messages via letters handed off between the low-ranking and unremarkable servants, such as the laundry maids and scullery maids, and during that exchange we came up with this plan.

Yes, I was a lady's maid. Mariel would be my mistress, of course. That was the plan.

A lady's maid was in the upper ranks of the servantry and had quite a lot of privileges even at a young age. They received comparatively special treatment, and had authority over personal matters beyond that of an average housekeeper. It wouldn't be out of the ordinary for one to be around her mistress at all times, and it was easy to maneuver in such a position.

And beyond that...

Francette, Roland, and Emile were cavalry guards. Belle was a nursemaid. Layette was a...nursed maid?

...Wait, what the heck is that?!

No, her role was to be nursed by Belle. I just made that up right now. And what's more...

Ed and the four others were our riding horses and substitutes. We had riding horses for House Raphael's guards, as well as horses for the carriage that Mariel and her servants would be using. There were many volunteer dogs and horses, so I picked out a team of elites.

All right, our preparations for the assault on the capital are complete!

...No, not really. I...absolutely cannot attack the capital with this team.

Since Mariel had been summoned by her faction leader, it was a given that he would use her as the star attraction to indicate to the aristocrats, royalty, and members of the Temple of the Goddess that the favor of the Goddess was with his faction.

So, just how much could they say? He was obviously planning on making Mariel spit out everything she knew, so she was likely worried about what she would do if he laid on the pressure.

Chapter 38: To the Capital

She couldn't put her own house or Count Maslias in a difficult position after all he had done for her, and she couldn't afford to be at odds with the leader of her faction, the royal family, or the Temple of the Goddess. That would be quite troubling...

I decided to join Mariel on her visit to the royal capital undercover out of a desire to help her, because I didn't want her blabbing about me, and because I wanted to squish the insects that plotted to harm Layette.

...Along with the hand-picked army of dogs and birds that were dying to join me.

Of course, we were all in disguise as Mariel's guards and servants to avoid suspicion. It was pointless to try to keep the House Raphael Expedition Corps from standing out, so I had given up on that at the start.

...A carriage surrounded by dozens of dogs with various species of birds flying over it, with each of the animals patrolling and sweeping its perimeter, couldn't hope to be the slightest bit inconspicuous.

Ahaha...

I had the others ride a separate carriage. Mariel, Belle, Layette, and I were in my carriage, and I desperately tried to dodge Mariel's barrage of questions, complaining to Belle that it took away my opportunity to spend time with Layette. Ed went ballistic on me during breaks for not riding him, so that was great...

And so, the day before we arrive at the capital...

There they are. They finally showed up. A group of bandits had been waiting for us, even though it was extremely rare for anyone to be dumb enough to attack a guarded carriage that obviously belonged to the nobility.

Attacking aristocrats so close to the capital all but guaranteed they would be met with brutal retaliation from the noble house that had been attacked, along with the royal family and capital army, both of whose reputations would be slighted.

If they let such brigands do as they pleased, even more aristocratic carriages would be attacked, they would be looked down upon by the other noble houses, and the number of vehicles going to the capital would decrease drastically, including those from merchants.

In addition…

"There are a bunch of people lined up in front of them!" One of the birds flew in from ahead and stopped on the carriage to deliver the message.

Oho…

"Call for the others. Prepare for bombardment!"

"Got it!"

"Scenario 1-C, is it?"

"Yeah, probably. Let's respond with number two in case it isn't C."

"Understood!"

After I informed Mariel of our intended response, she blew a whistle.

Our carriage slowed down, and our guards on horseback drew in closer. The dogs also gathered around the carriage, and the birds flew into the carriage one by one when the door opened.

"Okay, don't go overboard, now. Just carry whatever you can."

I brought out spheres with a thin film and glass balls, with handles on them to make them easier to hold for birds, and they each grasped one by the handle and flew off.

We'd practiced many times, so they took off without any issues.

All right, let's do this!

Chapter 38: To the Capital

"Stop! Stop, or we'll kill all…"

Slash!

Ah… Francette rushed in with incredible speed, then cut down the bandits at the front, who had seemed to be issuing a threat.

Well, he did say he was going to kill us, so they were definitely bandits and this was absolutely just self-defense.

"Y-You…"

Wsh!

"What the! L-Listen…"

Fwsh!

"Listen to…"

Stab! Slash! Slash!

Oh, there go Roland, Emile, and Mariel's guards too. They were like fish biting at every cast of the line… Well, maybe not exactly. In any case, the bandits got cut down rather one-sidedly, one by one. They were just completely outclassed…

"Th-This isn't what I signed up for! Wait, stop, pleeease!!!"

Slash! Swsh! Fsh!

There had been over twenty bandits to start with, but now only about half remained. Then…

"Run! Retreat! Retreeeat!!!" the man who seemed to be the leader of the bandits shouted.

…But their escape had been cut off.

"You're not going anywhere! Hmhm. Heheheheh…"

Francette, you sound like a villain…

"They're moving!" a messenger from the bird troops alerted me. It was a plain-colored and unassuming little bird.

"All right, begin the attack!"

"Got it!" the messenger answered and flew off energetically.

Now it was time to finish this.

"Hey everyone, don't forget to capture about half of them, okay? To all you bandits, we decided to kill anyone who resists and take those who surrender captive, so it's your choice!"

Clang, clang, clang!

Huh, all the remaining bandits dropped their weapons. How pathetic...

Meanwhile...

Boom, bang, boooooom!

"Aaahhhhhh!!!"

The platoon of infantry and about ten mounted soldiers who had been on standby rushed out, now that they had been called to action, but explosions suddenly erupted on the ground before them. Their horses abruptly changed directions or stopped in their tracks, causing complete chaos.

...Indeed, the glass balls, filled with something like nitroglycerin, had been dropped from the sky.

In addition...

Splish. Plsh, splash, splash...

Something soft landed on the soldiers.

"Blaaaaaargh!!!"

An unholy stench emanated from among them. The soldiers vomited violently. The horses went half-mad, trying to buck the soldiers from their backs, as they were the source of the horrid smell.

One after another, the birds landed the terrible-smelling fluids, each enclosed in a container of thin film, on the soldiers, then regained altitude to soar back into the sky. Afterward, they confirmed the results of their bombardment, and then flew away.

The soldiers couldn't calm the horses down, and they couldn't even get near their targets with such a god-awful smell on them. If they tried to force their way closer, the horses on the other side

Chapter 38: To the Capital

would start going crazy, too. Not to mention, they could be mistaken for attackers themselves, and no one would let them get anywhere close smelling like this. Anyone who approached you smelling like that had to have ill intentions.

And once the target approached them, they stood blocking the road, looking extremely suspicious...

It went without saying that they were assumed to be enemies. There was no way anyone would listen to their explanations or agree to travel with them otherwise.

It would have been one thing if they were emissaries of the king himself, but some noble house's personal guards had no authority to order a bunch of aristocrats around. Anyone who did such a thing couldn't really complain if they were immediately recognized as hostiles and consequently attacked.

"Damn it, what's going on?! The orders, these explosions, the birds, and this horrible-smelling bird crap... None of it makes sense! We were supposed to fend off the bandits attacking some nobles without killing or injuring them, then escort them to the capital... It was all a charade... Maybe all this scheming has upset the Goddess and... Wait, don't tell me...!"

The commander's face immediately paled. He had heard many stories of what happened to those who upset the Goddess Celestine. If those were true stories rather than myths...

This commander had also heard of the Goddess's miracles that recently happened in a certain city. He hadn't considered that this had anything to do with that incident, since he hadn't been given any additional details along with his orders. However, when he mentioned the Goddess's displeasure in his frustration, another situation beyond comprehension, involving aristocrats and birds, flashed in his mind.

"Bird aristocrat... N-No, abort mission! Get away from the road, quickly! Hide somewhere out of view!!!" the commander shouted, raising his voice in a panic, then moved away from the road and into the woods, pulling at his resisting horse...

"The humans up ahead have retreated."

"Thanks. Keep an eye on them to make sure they don't try anything funny with us, okay?"

"As you wish."

The messenger this time was a bigger bird. Maybe they had sent a bird with a bigger brain capacity; that is, a smart one, in case I had specific instructions. This one should be able to understand more complex orders... Wait, why was it so smart? I thought they called them "birdbrains" for a reason! This is all because Celes had forced knowledge into my head, in order to make the ability to comprehend all languages possible... No, I shouldn't think about it!

Chapter 38: To the Capital

"My lady, it appears the soldiers ahead of us have moved aside. Chances of them letting us pass without harassment: 70%. Chances of them appearing to make contact with us: 20%. Chances of them attacking us...should be below 10%, I believe."

"I see... Then let's proceed," Mariel said, nodding in response to my made-up calculations as she made her decision. Then Belle relayed Mariel's message to the driver, which the driver passed on to the other carriages and guards via whistle signals.

The eight bandits who had been captured had been stowed tied up in the carriage. We had already gone through a lot of food, fodder and other consumables, and it wasn't like we were a merchant caravan. Aristocratic passenger carriages weren't going to be filled to the brim with supplies. The carriages for the attendants and guards had a good amount of room, and could fit about eight people. ...And there was no need to consider comfort for these captives.

In any case, there were currently five people riding in my carriage.

Me, Mariel, Belle, Layette...and one bandit. Yes, one of them was riding in the same carriage as us.

"It's time for your questioning! Let's have some fun, shall we?!"

Oh, maybe I should get rid of that smell.

They had just followed their superiors' orders, so I felt bad about that stench soaking into their expensive equipment...

I decided to spray a smell-neutralizing agent when we passed by them. Making it appear in the form of mist, without a container and directly above them, should do the trick.

Yup, you can't forget the spirit of benevolence.

"Hm... So the plan was to stop us, then when the soldiers came riding in while you were threatening us, you were supposed to run away without harming anyone..."

Nod, nod, nod.

"So you were in cahoots with those soldiers, then?"

"I-I don't know about that... Our boss was killed, and we were just doing what he told us to..." The bandit in our carriage told us everything he knew.

For some reason, he became extremely cooperative when I said, "If you don't talk, I can just kill you and talk to someone else."

Now that their leader had died and all their surviving comrades had been captured, there was no reason for them to try to act noble or keep secrets. There was no denying that they were bandits, and it was no surprise that they chose to cooperate in hopes of finding better work as judicial slaves, ideally somewhere other than in the mines.

And if they knew what was going on, they could get off easier just by saying, "We were just told to act like we were going to attack a group of people, and we aren't real bandits. We're just some thugs who got hired for money." They might get off with a lighter punishment this way, so there was no reason for them to keep any secrets at this point. ...That meant that only their dead boss actually knew anything of value.

...I messed up. I should have captured their leader alive...

But I didn't even know who their leader was at that point, and we didn't have much of a choice other than cutting them down without hesitation. Francette would've been fine, but the other guards could have been injured or killed otherwise. ...That went for Roland and Emile, too.

Chapter 38: To the Capital

Besides, it was highly likely that, even if we had gotten the leader's testimony, it would likely have been dismissed as a self-serving lie, and he'd end up getting silenced via assassination.

Well, it wasn't like they had plotted to hurt Mariel, and they really just wanted to make her owe them as a way in, so it wasn't too much of an offense.

And to find the real culprit behind all this, I didn't have to ask the bandits, who might have not even told the truth. …There wasn't even any guarantee that their client gave the bandits their real name.

It was pretty standard practice to use the name of an aristocrat from an opposing faction when hiring criminals. I had to go with something more foolproof.

Yes, I had about three birds tracking them. I wanted to find out where and who those soldiers were reporting to.

Crows are very intelligent creatures. They can recognize individual humans and remember them for quite a long time. So, I wasn't expecting too much, but if things went right, I had a chance of finding out who put these bandits up to this…

"We've arrived," Mariel said, as she finished watching the road ahead with her head out of the window, and withdrew back inside.

The rest of us took turns poking our heads out of the window, finding long stretches of stone walls to either side, a townscape of stone buildings, and a building that looked like some sort of castle or temple.

…It was the nation's capital, which is why it was defended by its castle walls that surrounded its entire perimeter.

"Whoaaa, so big…" Layette was right. It was far bigger than the only other major city in this country, the one where Layette's Atelier was located — the capital city of Litenia in the Kingdom of Jusral.

Commerce was thriving because merchants were powerful here, which meant they had a strong economy, which likely was the reason they had grown so big. ...It seemed it was pretty different from the countries that focused on powerful militaries.

But you couldn't have a lot of military power without economic power.

Actually, there were some places that used most of their national budget on their military despite being poor. So maybe the size of the capital and the impressiveness of its castle walls weren't an indicator of a country's overall power.

Hmm... So complicated...

...Okay, I'm done thinking about this.

It was just a waste of time.

Now, what to do once we get to the capital...

Mariel's group, which included us, would be guests at the capital residence of House Raphael's parent house, House Maslias.

A poor viscount couldn't afford a capital residence. We would normally stay at a fancy inn for aristocrats, but we couldn't do that this time.

If we got a room at an inn as soon as we arrived in the capital, it would be asking for everyone from nobles, merchants, religious folks, and people looking to get rich quick to come storming the building to talk to Mariel, who was known as the Bird Aristocrat and the Goddess's beloved child. We couldn't count on the aristocrats from her faction either. In fact, they would probably be even worse.

So Count Maslias insisted that we stay at his capital residence instead, for her safety rather than for financial reasons. No one disagreed with his reasoning.

That meant Mariel and the others should be safe for now. Though, that didn't cover any time she would spend meeting with

Chapter 38: To the Capital

other nobles from her faction, or when they took her to the royal palace, temple, or some big-time merchant's place...

Of course, we would be with her as her attendants and guards if that did happen. We were using up the limited slots for the number of people she could bring with her, so we had to fulfill our duty. Besides, I had requested to come with her in the first place so I could give her support if she ever needed it.

Even though I did what I did to help Mariel, per Carlos's request, this had all happened because of me, so I had to deal with the aftermath...

Well, that was actually fine. I just had to deal with whatever came at her. The problem was the main reason I decided to come to the capital as Mariel's support.

Yes, I still needed to find out who hurt Layette and have a "conversation" with them.

It would have been fine if they had gone for me.

If they had targeted me directly, I would have just wiped them out and dealt the finishing blow. I would have been satisfied with inflicting a fatal wound.

But the people that went after my friends that I hold dear...

The people who injured and nearly killed those orphans...

They're done for.

They had made moves against us in that city. Now that Mariel was here, a person who was thought to have been in contact with the Angel they were after, there was no way they wouldn't try something.

And no one would suspect that the so-called Angel herself would be with her the whole time.

There would be folks who'd try to take Mariel in and use her.

If there was anyone among them who seemed more interested in the Angel rather than Mariel herself and tried to get information out of her...

I will crush them. ...Squish them like grapes.

And I would do it in such a way that no one would ever fathom trying anything with the Angel or anyone around her. It would need to be a truly fear-inducing method, with plenty of publicity around it...

There was no need to send a message to the general public.

Most people had absolutely no intention of slighting Celes or anyone related to her.

But there were fools who thought they could take advantage of friends of the Goddess just because they had a little bit of money and authority.

When they catch a whiff of what I had planned in their information networks that they had built with all their money and power...

Haha.

Hahahahaha!

"We're about to cross through the city gates."

Okay, I was tripping out a little there... Belle had to pull me back to reality.

In any case, we were finally arriving at the capital.

Of course, the line of aristocratic carriages didn't have to go through an examination upon entering the gates.

A retainer had gone ahead to take care of the procedures so that the carriages could pass through without halting. A guide from Count Maslias's household who had been waiting for us guided us in.

The Raphael household knew where Count Maslias's house was located, but this move not only served as a sort of welcoming ceremony for important guests, but also prevented anyone from intercepting Mariel on her way to Count Maslias's place.

Chapter 38: To the Capital

Stopping a line of carriages that were being led by the host would not only be outrageously discourteous, but one could be assumed to be hostile and attacked immediately for doing so. Not only that, but the leader and those involved would be executed.

That was the obvious punishment for attacking aristocrats in the capital. It would dishonor the king, the leading aristocrats, and every influential merchant and reserve soldier in the capital, so even a high-ranking aristocrat wouldn't escape unscathed.

...And so, this bug repellant was working like a charm.

As expected, there were several people who looked like "the type" staring with resentment at the lead horse and two mounted guards, each featuring Count Maslias's crest, as well as the line of House Raphael's carriages.

Count Maslias was very lenient when it came to Mariel, but he took the proper measures against other influential aristocrats.

It seemed that I would be able to focus all of my resources on luring out my enemy without having to divert any of my forces to protect Mariel while she was under Count Maslias's care.

...As such thoughts crossed my mind, Belle spoke up.

"I don't think there are very many people who are brave enough to try something with all those dogs around us and birds overhead."

Huh, so, those expressions on their faces weren't resentful, but dumbfounded and astonished.

Well, whatever. It didn't make much difference.

And so, we arrived at the capital residence of Count Maslias.

Count Maslias had arranged things with various departments for us beforehand, and now welcomed us upon arrival.

Someone had gone ahead to give them advance notice of our arrival, and Mariel was led straight to the bath that had been readied for her.

A servant from the count's household tried to attend to her while she was bathing, but Mariel vehemently refused. Mariel's own attendants ended up going with her instead.

...Yes, that was me, along with Belle and Layette.

Mariel had done this out of courtesy, figuring we wouldn't have the chance to take a bath if she let the count's attendants take care of her.

I mean, no aristocrat would let a servant bathe in a bath intended for their important guests...

Apparently, Mariel couldn't stand the thought of getting to take a bath while we would only get to wipe ourselves down with a towel using sink water.

...Though, that was understandable.

Even though I was pretending to be her servant and Mariel was playing along pretty well, there was no way she could stomach that when she thought I was a goddess. She was only going through this act and taking it so seriously in the first place because I told her that this was necessary and the will of the Goddess.

And so, she used this opportunity to say she wanted me to attend to her bath so we could go in there with her. Belle and Layette were thus able to enjoy the benefits, as well.

To be honest, I was thankful, so, I decided to accept Mariel's generosity.

...And I pretended not to hear the creepy voice saying, *"Bathing together with the Goddess... Kehe... Kehehe..."*

Chapter 38: To the Capital

Francette was our knightly guard, so it would have been a bit of a stretch to get her in too. I felt bad for her, but she was gonna have to sit this one out. There were no hard feelings, really. It couldn't be helped.

...I don't want to talk about bathing anymore.
I'm never taking a bath with Mariel again.

Once we were done bathing, it was time to meet up with Count Maslias to work out a plan of attack. The meeting's participants were the count, his two subordinates, Mariel, me, Belle, and Layette. Belle was with me as my guard, and I only brought Layette because I couldn't just leave her alone. Those two didn't actually have anything to do with the meeting.

Seeing the three of us in attendance, the count gave us a dubious expression, and I honestly couldn't blame him. As the lady's maid, maybe me being there wouldn't have been completely ridiculous, but he must have been confused by the presence of Belle the nursemaid and Layette the nursed maid. We had Francette, Roland, and Emile stay out of it because it would have been unnatural for mere guards to be in the meeting, but this pretty much defeated the purpose of doing so.

Well, we had too many people from our side, so I had no choice but to exclude those three, anyway.

"...Hm? You there..."

Huh, did the count recognize me?

"Ah, yes, I've met you at Ma... Viscountess Raphael's house."

Crap, I almost said "at Mariel's place"!

The servants at House Raphael called her different things, whether "my lady," "Lady Mariel," or "Miss Mariel," so it should be fine. He would probably just assume I was about to say "my lady" and corrected myself when I realized we weren't at home.

"After that incident, I took note of her wisdom and hired her as a lady's maid. I'm sure she will be a great help for us," Mariel said, and the count seemed to accept that.

"Hm, what was it you called yourself? A di...det..."

"I am the one who seeks and investigates truth. A detective, sir."

One truth prevails!

And so, the meeting began.

Thanks to Mariel supporting me when the count realized who I was, I was acknowledged as Mariel's advisor rather than as an ordinary lady's maid, so I was granted the right to give my input in this meeting...I think. That's what it felt like, anyway. That was some unexpected luck!

And so, the discussion *really* began...

According to the viscount, the so-called leader of the faction that called Mariel to the capital was on top of the world right now. This country had various political and business circles, from the royal court faction with the king at its top, the merchants' faction with the Commerce Guild at their back, the religious faction that had integrated itself with the Temple of the Goddess. Then there was a mid-level noble faction that didn't really stand out too much. That was the faction that Count Maslias and House Raphael belonged to.

Chapter 38: To the Capital

A "beloved child of the Goddess" had appeared from a noble house within his faction, which was quite a big deal. Apparently, he was pretty excited about the thought of using this opportunity to increase his influence and eventually expanding his faction to the greatest heights possible.

Ah…

And so, he had been scheming…I mean, planning all sorts of ways to use Mariel as a publicity tool to increase his influence.

I mean, the beloved child of the Goddess sounded a lot more appealing than the royal family, which were ordinary people who were just descendants of people who happened to be kings a long time ago. These people have never performed miracles or had connections with the Goddess or received her visions. She would be very enticing to the nobles, the temple, the merchants, and even the common people…

It was no wonder they were making such a big deal out of her.

"The faction leader, Marquis Cedric, is planning to take Mariel around to the Temple of the Goddess and the merchants in order to lure them into his own faction, regardless of their occupations. Of course, this includes the lower and mid-class nobles directly related to them, as well…"

That was a pretty standard strategy for someone who had obtained a ridiculously powerful weapon…

"And of course, the other factions would do anything to claim Mariel as one of their own. If it came down to it, they'd try to take me along with her. Hahaha…" the count said, laughing dryly.

The other factions seemed to assume that the relationship between Count Maslias and House Raphael was just that of a parent house and the house under it, and that Mariel didn't have any particular loyalty toward Count Maslias, due to having just taken her seat as the head of the household. They likely didn't even imagine that he had taken care of her since childhood, and that she had remarkable devotion to and trust in him.

And regarding the idea of taking in the entire count's household with her, I couldn't comment without knowing his current standing within his faction and how he had gotten there. But judging from the weak smile the count was putting on, it seemed he didn't have the power to influence the faction in any meaningful way.

"And it's not just the various factions of aristocrats vying for Mariel, but the royal palace and Temple of the Goddess also want her as their own, and the merchants are desperate to get in contact with her to secure their financial gain. When Mariel meets with Marquis Cedric, I will be in attendance, as the head of her parent house and her guardian, but I can't be there when he takes her around the city. If he tries to have her commit to any unfavorable promises…"

"You want us to support her, I presume?"

"Yes, I'm counting on you. And do be wary of any talks involving marriage, sponsoring domains, becoming a shrine maiden, attending parties at the royal palace, or marriage," the count said, pressing the point further.

…But why did he mention marriage twice? Was it really that important?

Our meeting with the count continued for some time before breaking up. We had what seemed to be the epitome of an aristocrat's dinner, then each of us retired to our rooms. Mariel later told me nobles didn't actually have dinners like one this every night. Only for special occasions and when guests were over.

…I guess that should've been obvious. Forget about the expenses; if anyone ate like this every night, they'd get sick and die early! Since I was a servant, I didn't get my own room, of course, but shared one with Layette and Belle.

...The guys? Who knows.

Belle strongly insisted that she have the privilege of sleeping with Layette, so I let her. I could sleep with Layette whenever I wanted, after all. As a knight, Francette wasn't one to let her guard down in foreign territory. Apparently, she was going to move the desk to the door, put a vase on it, then sit under the window and sleep with one knee up and her sword in her arms.

...Yeah, I figured.

When I awoke the next day, the table in front of the door had already been returned to its original place, and Francette stared into my eyes with her sheathed sword in her left hand.

...Our faces were about ten centimeters apart.

That's kinda freaky! I actually screamed out loud!

I ended up lecturing her not to do it ever again, but she seemed unhappy about that.

Damn it, I'll do the same thing to her next time! Let's see how you like the feeling of your heart stopping!

Chapter 38: To the Capital

Breakfast time.

It was quite a lot of food. People woke up early in this world, and farmers, hunters, woodcutters, and people who went on journeys or had to prepare their lunch out in the field couldn't spend too much time preparing their meals, much less ingredients or water. Of course, that included soldiers who were operating outdoors. So eating a big breakfast and a simple lunch, then taking the time to enjoy an early dinner with their friends was the standard practice.

...Yeah, as someone who's used to the Japanese style, I still couldn't get used to huge breakfasts even after being here for five years. Well, I had usually made my own breakfast during that time, so I still ate light in the morning like most people in Japan did. As such, I never did get used to how they did morning meals here.

But when aristocrats ate with guests over, it was normal to serve a boatload of food and leave whatever they couldn't finish, so it was no problem if I didn't finish it all.

"That only applies to Lady Mariel and the other aristocrats! It's customary for us servants to finish whatever we are served!" Francette pointed out.

We had been invited to the feast last night as a token of appreciation and to put Mariel at ease, but of course, the servants and mistress didn't dine together after that.

...Yeah, I had expected that. So, I had no choice but to swap it with Francette's pretty-much-empty plate of food.

...*Don't give me that exasperated look! You're not fuel-efficient, so I know you need more food. This is a win-win for us!*

And so, we all went to the faction leader's place together.

...All of us except Belle and Layette, that is.

113

Unlike me, the lady's maid, and Francette, Mariel's guard (and able to stay near Mariel even while she was changing or out picking flowers), it would be quite a stretch to ask for the nursed maid to come along…

Roland and Emile joined as guards for the carriage, and would wait in the next room during meetings in case something happened. When the faction leader took Mariel around in a few days, Francette and I would be the only ones who could accompany her, at best. If we tried to bring some other man as a guard, it would be like saying we didn't trust the faction leader or his own guards' abilities. That would have been too much of a slight for him to ignore.

Chapter 39: Negotiations

"Ah, welcome! I am Marquis Cedric!"

Marquis Cedric was the leader of the faction that House Maslias and House Raphael belonged to. He was past sixty, which was still a healthy age in modern Japan, but he was considered quite old here. His skin was pretty wrinkly, too.

According to Count Maslias, Marquis Cedric had taken up the role of faction leader, a role that had been passed down for generations, but he had no particular ambitions or drive to speak of, and was nothing more than the organizer of a small, temperate faction with middle-of-the-road political views. ...Or he had been until last month, that is.

He had started getting carried away ever since the beloved daughter of the Goddess Celestine had appeared in his faction. Not only was she young, cute, and unmarried, but she was also the head of a noble house; it was basically like pulling a triple *yakuman* or a royal flush.

It wasn't like he was looking to conquer the world, but he had begun plotting great advancements for his faction. No, I'm not saying that's necessarily a bad thing. As a politician and faction leader, it's only natural for him to strive for more power and to push the policies he believes in for the benefit of his faction's nobles and his country.

…At least, it wouldn't have been a problem if it hadn't involved nasty tactics like taking advantage of a little girl. So there you have it.

And so, the marquis's attack had begun! The marquis didn't seem to have any intention of doing anything to Mariel himself in his old age, but he was going to try to get her closer to his grandson and the influential aristocrats from his faction, and mentioned those parties with obvious intentions…

However, Mariel gracefully evaded such invitations by saying that she wasn't ready for any such thing, because she was still grieving from the loss of her family, or otherwise because she needed to focus on sorting out the confusion in her domain first.

The marquis hurled words at Mariel like spears, one after another, and she deftly dodged each one in a dance of words.

Whoa… Can't underestimate these nobles!

Mariel evaded the marquis's invitation to stay at his residence on a more long-term basis by saying that she needed to prioritize getting to know her domain after taking over as head of her household, but even she couldn't refuse his request to meet the other nobles of the faction, visit the royal palace, or stop by and see some influential merchants. These weren't requests to Mariel on an individual level, but official requests that were part of her duties as the head of the Raphael household.

And when she began to fulfill her duties starting tomorrow, she wouldn't have any supporting fire from Count Maslias at her back.

"I'm tired…"

The battle finally ended, and only then were we allowed to leave. It was pretty amazing that all Mariel had to say about all this was that she was tired.

Chapter 39: Negotiations

"Well, it's important to keep a good relationship with the marquis. Otherwise, Mariel would be in opposition to the entire faction. If she loses the shield supporting her, she would be swarmed by all sorts of adversaries at once…"

Count Maslias was right. We couldn't afford to antagonize Maslias Cedric right off the bat. If he had just been a regular member of the faction, having a personal disagreement with him wouldn't have been a big issue. It was common for aristocrats to have opposing interests, so even those in the same faction weren't all going to be all buddy-buddy with each other. You just had to make sure to take care of the key points.

…And we had just dealt with that part.

Now we just had to make sure to accommodate the nobles that treated us favorably, and completely avoid anyone who might be potentially harmful. It wasn't that I had something against the faction itself, but we had to keep a distance from any faction members who harbored ill will toward us. This was more of an issue on an individual level between noble houses, so it didn't have anything to do with the faction as a whole.

In any case, the rest was up to Mariel. I didn't know what the opposing aristocrats and Marquis Cedric were planning, but that wasn't a big concern.

…Why do you think Francette and I were gonna be by Mariel's side?

"Ah, welcome! Please, right this way…"

The next day, we — that is, the trio of me, Mariel, and Francette — were led by Marquis Cedric and his subordinates and guards to visit the nobles of the faction. Honestly, it would've gone a lot quicker if we had just gathered everyone and met them at once.

That was my thought process, but apparently, that wouldn't work because we wouldn't have been able to do much else besides exchange quick greetings. According to them, that would have been a real shame after inviting Mariel all the way to the capital.

…That meant these visits were definitely for "that purpose." You know, the one that got mentioned twice.

"I am Viscountess Mariel von Raphael. Pleased to meet you…"

Everyone knew her name already, of course, but it was customary for her to introduce herself. As for us, the servant and guard, we didn't need to do anything of the sort.

Marquis Cedric quickly introduced the two sides to each other, then explained that Mariel had taken over as head of House Raphael and made some noncommittal comments about how she would remain in the faction just as her parents had been. He didn't mention anything about the Goddess at all.

That was a connection that everyone had to make on their own. This meeting was merely to introduce her as a new member of the faction, and it wasn't something they could pursue in front of Marquis Cedric. This time was to be spent making connections and establishing favorable relations as members of the same faction, to set up for when the appropriate time did come. Only a fool would make careless comments here.

And just as she'd been doing, Mariel met with them peacefully and without incident. Whoever put those bandits and knights up to that whole act wasn't among the nobles here. It wouldn't have made sense for someone with the advantage of being in the same faction and having actual opportunities to meet with Mariel right away to take such risks. That was the type of scheme that would be cooked up by someone who wouldn't be able to meet her otherwise.

…And I already knew who the culprit was.

Chapter 39: Negotiations

The birds had already secretly trailed those knights, but since birds couldn't read the words on signs, I had them lead Emile there to confirm the owner of the manor. But I wasn't too concerned about them. Their methods had been a bit underhanded, but they weren't particularly malicious or hostile.

Although they had hired bandits, it was only for the purpose of putting Mariel in their debt as a means of getting close to her. It wasn't as if they meant any real harm. Now that their original plan had failed, they would likely try to make contact with her some other way. It would probably be another somewhat underhanded tactic, like making us feel like we were in danger without actually hurting us, and swooping in to the rescue right after...

That didn't bother me.

...But I did plan on confronting them and talking them down. If we could dig up some dirt on the other nobles, it would give Mariel an edge she needed. Honestly, this was kinda fun. It was like a PVP game.

...The real problem was the other group. The group that had hired the thugs who beat the orphans half to death and hurt Layette. I'll never forgive them! They may think they've gotten away with it, but I'm not gonna let that fly. The day has eyes, and the night has ears!

"I am Viscountess Mariel von Raphael. Pleased to meet you..." she said to the next aristocrat.

It was a count this time. The introduction went on like the other ones, but...

"I hear you will be coming of age soon, viscountess? And that you have been receiving education as the head of your noble house since abruptly becoming the heir and successor... It seems to me that you must find a husband, so as to bring stability to your house as soon as possible. So, perhaps you would consider my son? My second and third sons are also learned in the ways of managing a domain, so you could leave it all up to any of them!"

Yeah, this wasn't surprising, considering he had his wife and kids with him, too, but none of the other aristocrats had gone about it so blatantly. The others just casually mentioned that their son was close to Mariel in age, at most.

"Oh, but I've just recently lost my parents and brother, so I can't bring myself to think about that right now… I think I will still be mourning for some time…"

Mariel cast one of her denial spells she had prepared beforehand. All of the aristocrats that came at her with the previously mentioned reserved approach backed off at this point.

"Ah, but it's precisely at times like these that you must get yourself a dependable husband to handle the management of your domain! Then you can focus on your political engagements to ensure the prosperity of your family and faction…"

Yes, yes, and by "your family," you mean your son's family; in other words, your own.

Mariel had incredible name value as the child who was blessed and loved by the Goddess, but even without that, she would have been an attractive marriage candidate.

If she had just been the daughter of a viscount, neither the head of the house or the successor, she would have been the one seeking a house to marry into. But since she was a viscountess, another aristocrat would seek to give her his second or third son. And if she was to birth him a grandson, the house would become his completely. After that, it wouldn't matter to him if Mariel was to die of an illness or in an accident.

Chapter 39: Negotiations

She even came with the bonus of being the beloved child of the Goddess. There was no way they wouldn't be after her. Not to mention, a child born from the beloved child of the Goddess even had a chance of marrying into the royal family. In fact, that was very well within the realm of possibility.

No wonder they were so desperate to get her…

"I'm certain the count and Viscountess Raphael still need time for things to settle. Perhaps it would be better to discuss such matters on another day…"

Marquis Cedric decided to step in as the faction leader and the coordinator for this meeting. It seemed he was fulfilling his role properly.

"Nonsense! You will be taking her to the temple and royal palace tomorrow, will you not?! Of course they will try to take the viscountess for themselves! It will be much easier to avoid their attempts if we say she is already betrothed!"

…It seemed the count had no intention of backing off. Well, he wasn't wrong. The royal palace and Temple of the Goddess could indeed try to take Mariel in directly, which was much quicker and more efficient than waiting for her to have a daughter. It was understandable for the count to be worried. But that didn't mean she had any obligation to marry the count's son.

"Oh, please don't worry about that. I have no intention of marrying anyone from the Temple of the Goddess, anyone in the royal palace, or your children."

"You mustn't say such selfish things! It is a noble daughter's duty to marry for the good of their household! Regardless of your own will, you should marry whoever the head of the house…"

"Yes, and I intend to do just that. …As the head of my house, I will decide who to marry."

The count trailed off, realizing what he had said. Yeah, he'd screwed up.

"Uh, but since you are not yet of age, you should obey your faction leader, Marquis Cedric! Isn't that right, Marquis?!"

I was starting to get really annoyed by this count's persistence.

...But it seemed Mariel was getting even more annoyed than I was. There was a smile on her face, but... Let's just say that I could see a vein popping out on her temple. Then, Mariel bent her right pointer finger with a repeated beckoning motion.

...It was the signal that meant, "Get him!"

Oh, Mariel, if you insist... Here goes, Wrath of the Goddess!

Boom! Pop! Bam!

Suddenly, the vases and ornaments on the furniture exploded and shattered into pieces.

"Aaahhhhhh!!!"

The marquis, the count, and the count's wife and two children dove from the sofa and rolled behind us, away from the explosion. Mariel quickly stood up, looked about thirty degrees up into the air, put her hands together in front of her and shouted.

"Please, Goddess, there is no need to murder the count's entire family or destroy his domain for this... It isn't the time for such measures quite yet..."

"G... G? Gyaaaaaaaaagh!!!"

Yeah, Mariel wasn't here to start any fires. The opposite, in fact; she had come to the capital to preemptively snuff out any commotion or trouble while it was still just starting to smolder. And her method of putting out fires was to...

Well, are you familiar with how they extinguish fires in oil fields? They stick some dynamite in there and blow away the flames with the explosion!

Chapter 39: Negotiations

"..." Marquis Cedric sat quietly during our carriage ride to the next faction noble's manor, looking pale.

I mean, he had just seen firsthand what happened when you tried to force Mariel to do something she didn't want to. He was probably praising himself for not having done anything like that during their meeting yesterday, and likely praying that tomorrow's visits to the temple and royal palace would go without incident, or that he would at least be able to get through them safely.

We finished the rest of the meetings without any issues, and the aristocrats who had their sons with them never even brought up the topic of marriages or engagements, for some reason. I didn't know whether that had anything to do with the fact that Marquis Cedric had pulled one of the mounted guards aside and whispered something to him, shortly before that guard rode off somewhere as fast as he could. Yup.

The following day...

It was a doubleheader kind of day, with the visit to the Temple of the Goddess in the morning and the royal palace in the afternoon. Or maybe it was an irregular doubleheader, since the enemy team was going to change midway through. And this was an away game, not a home game. But as a game, it wasn't like the sum of everyone's interests totaled zero; in other words, the amount in the pie that would be distributed wasn't predetermined, so it wasn't a zero-sum game.

...So, there were ways that everyone could end up happy, but there were ways that everyone could end up unhappy, too. However, that excluded Mariel. Maybe it wasn't appropriate to compare this to a game, but Mariel was more like an employee of the company running the game, rather than a player, so she couldn't lose.

The visit to the royal palace would be later because we had already visited the faction's nobles yesterday, so we could prioritize the temple today and claim we had started at the bottom and worked our way up to the top.

On the other hand, we could tell the temple that we had prioritized them over the royal palace. I could tell Marquis Cedric had really thought this through. We normally wouldn't have to worry about such things, but since this involved the beloved child of the Goddess, there were all sorts of things like the power dynamics at play that had to be considered. It wasn't easy being a working adult, and a mid-level manager at that…

In any case, we arrived at the Temple of the Goddess.

The question was, what sort of position did the temple consider the beloved child of the Goddess to occupy? Did they see her as only a little girl who had just happened to receive the blessing of the Goddess, and thus consider her lower than a priest? Or was she like the Goddess and Angel, who were above priests, who after all were merely human? And how did the fact that she was an aristocrat affect the temple's ranking system?

I've only played the role of a goddess and the Angel, so I didn't know much about her so-called beloved children. It wasn't like Mariel knew anyone like that herself, so she didn't know either.

…In fact, maybe the people at the temple didn't know either. It was like an SSR (Special Super Rare) card that had never appeared before.

Well, well, what would happen now…?

Wait, whoa!

The members of the Temple of the Goddess all appeared in a row to greet us.

It appeared the beloved child (Mariel) was an UL (Ultra Legend)…

Chapter 39: Negotiations

"Thank you for coming. We of the Temple of the Goddess wholeheartedly welcome you…"

One of the bishops had led us to this room, and an archbishop greeted us with those words of welcome. This was the person who held the highest religious rank within the capital, which also meant that he was the highest-ranking religious figure in this country. There had only been a pope and cardinal in the Holy Land of Rueda, but now that Rueda had been wiped out, those ranks no longer existed.

Well, some country out there may have appointed one on their own, but it wasn't like anyone would take that seriously. It would make much more sense to appoint one here rather than accept some random person from another country as pope. But then, they had witnessed the destruction of the Holy Land and the fall of their priests… And then there was us, with Celestine at our backs.

The temple surely had received accurate reports about that incident. They couldn't afford to do anything stupid here…

In any case, it seemed all the countries were now on equal grounds, with their own archbishops, without any issues.

…At least, that's how it seemed on the outside.

Of course, each country had their own relationship between the temple and royal palace, and there were differences in their political influences, financial situations, and the power of the countries themselves, so they were never truly equal, and there may have even been some archbishops vying to become pope out there.

Though, it seemed that truly evil priests were pretty rare. I mean, this was a world where a goddess actually existed, and divine punishment was a very real thing…

And an entire country had been destroyed for that very thing a little more than four years ago, and the priesthood there was still in shambles…

Actually, there was a case of divine punishment just a few days ago! There was no way anyone would plot to do evil when the very person involved in that incident was right here.

...Unless they were planning on picking a fight with the Goddess, that is.

It didn't seem possible that whoever was behind the attack on the orphans and Layette was related to the Temple of the Goddess. If it had been someone from the temple, they would know very well how dangerous it was to pick a fight with her. As such, the culprit was very likely to be someone who only had incomplete information, someone who didn't understand what the Angel was capable of, or someone who thought it was all a hoax and hoped to capitalize on it.

...Though, it was possible that they were just stupid.

Some inoffensive conversation went on for a while longer, then...

"What do you say, Viscountess Raphael? Would you consider becoming a priestess of our temple to serve Lady Celestine along with us...?"

There it is. Here we go...

And of course, Mariel's reply was...

"No, the Goddess did not help me so that I would become her priestess. She stopped House Raphael from being taken over by evil, and offered me her divine strength so I could become the true successor of my house and protect my domain. If I forsake my domain to become a priestess, I would be getting my priorities completely wrong. It would be betraying the Goddess's own kindness..."

Yup, that was a perfect response. There was no way a priest could counter that. And just as expected, the archbishop stood in silence, at a loss for words.

Chapter 39: Negotiations

Mariel only said "the Goddess" in her statement and never actually mentioned Celestine by name. If she had, that would've been a lie. The Goddess that Mariel was talking about was me, so as long as she phrased it that way, it was technically the truth.

...To her, anyway.

They still tried to tie her down, asking her to be an honorary priestess, to have her sign the temple's name list, to show up only during religious rites, or to get involved "just a little bit," but all such requests were shot down.

If she had agreed to be a priestess, even in name, they could have used her, and she'd be within their social hierarchy. As it was, she may have been a follower of Celestine, but she was still the normal head of a noble household, so she didn't have to follow orders from the Temple of the Goddess.

Aristocrats only had an obligation to follow their own beliefs and those orders from the king that they agreed with, so long as they weren't completely irrational or unfair. Even if the king tried to force an unreasonable order, nobles were often able to reject it, ask other aristocrats of their faction for help, or request help from powerful merchants they were close with. That was the whole point of having factions and keeping up exchanges with the merchants.

Well, this country's king had never been a dictator, most of its important policies were decided in meetings between influential nobles, and the merchants actually had a lot of sway here, so things were run somewhat differently compared to other places.

And so, we quickly left the archbishop behind as he watched us regretfully, knowing full well that he couldn't force us to do anything. It seemed Marquis Cedric wasn't so adept at dealing with the Temple of the Goddess, so he didn't say much during this visit, but Mariel handled it just as we had discussed beforehand.

And now, we just had the royal palace to deal with. This was probably going to be the most troublesome one.

The king here apparently had less authority compared to other countries, so he was more like the highest-ranking aristocrat rather than the actual king, or someone to fill a title that they needed solely to have someone in the same position as the kings of other realms during negotiations...

In any case, his position wasn't the same as a traditional king. This had probably been a normal kingdom before, but that's my understanding of how things were now.

...Maybe he would be easier to deal with if he didn't have that much authority? No, no, that would be all the more reason for him to cling desperately to such an opportunity. He would use anything he could to increase his power...

Anyway, we returned to the marquis's manor first to have some lunch.

We rested well afterward, then off to the royal palace we went...

"I-I'm actually starting to get nervous..." Mariel had been acting pretty unconcerned up until now, but her resolve seemed to weaken as we approached the front gates.

She may have been tough, but she was still a fourteen-year-old girl, so I couldn't really blame her. I figured I should give her some encouragement...

"I'm sure you will be fine! Sir Roland taught you all manner of things, did he not?"

"Y-Yes..."

Marquis Cedric was in the same carriage, so I had to talk in-character as a servant.

Mariel's cheeks turned pink at the mention of Roland's name.

Roland had joined the journey as a guard, but that really was purely a pretext. I had actually introduced him to Mariel as the guardian knight of the Goddess Kaoru and a gentleman of high status. I said something similar about Francette, too. So in Mariel's mind, Roland was someone who was far above her in social standing.

...I mean, he actually was. And he was needlessly attractive, so I couldn't blame Mariel for blushing.

...Yeah, not much I could do about that. Even if Francette was in somewhat of a bad mood because of it...

So, what Mariel had learned from Roland was, of course, how to deal with royals, how to interpret their behavior, what they were plotting when they did certain things, and other various anti-royal techniques. After all, if he wasn't going to be useful now, when was he ever?!

This is your only chance to shine, so you'd better make it count!

I had given him those words of encouragement, but he had been pretty down afterward. I wonder why... I was just telling him I had high expectations of him. Anyway, our preliminary training and Q&A simulation were perfect.

Roland was absent today, as were Emile, Belle, and Layette, but I told Mariel that Sir Roland was surely watching over her from afar, and she nodded with a determined look.

...I mean, Roland wasn't dead or anything, but Mariel wasn't familiar with Japanese phrases, so she probably interpreted it as him watching over her in a general sense.

And so, we arrived at the royal palace! We passed right through the front gates, thanks to the presence of the marquis and his family crest on the carriage. Once we got out of the carriage, the marquis led us into the room where we were to wait for an audience.

Chapter 39: Negotiations

There were a few other guests there before us, and it seemed that we were the last to be seen. I figured he would want to get through the others quickly and use the rest of the time for Mariel.

Francette was dressed like a maid today, matching my look, and the divine sword Exgram was inside my Item Box. It wasn't as if we could bring an armed guard in to see the king. Though, I would only need one second to pull the sword out of my Item Box and pass it to Francette. I doubted any situation would really change much within that one second.

...Hey, Fran. You're a maid right now, so stop looking around like you're ready to kill any threat!

And so, once the others were done with their audiences, it was Mariel's turn. Mariel and the count walked ahead in a line, and we followed shortly after, looking down so as to avoid staring directly at the king's face. But I'd been told this event was just for exchanging brief statements, and the real discussions would take place in another room.

...I guess that was to be expected. There was no way we could enjoy a hearty conversation with one knee on the ground while talking to a man leaning back in his fancy chair atop his platform, after all.

Some time later, we moved to a relatively smaller room, one that wasn't used for super-official discussions, and had our first real meeting; the others had mostly been cookie-cutter exchanges of pleasantries.

We were led into the room first, and after we stood there for some time, the king and several others who seemed to be his ministers and such also entered. We had entered the room in the opposite order from before, but that wasn't surprising. It wasn't like we could make the king wait for us.

"Welcome..."

He began to say something once seated, then trailed off when he looked over in our direction...or rather, when he looked at Francette and me standing behind Mariel and the count.

Yeah, he probably found it weird to find some seemingly unrelated people here. Of course he would. It was extremely unusual for a maid to attend a meeting like this. Normally, someone of such a low rank would stay in the waiting room.

Of course, the guards that guided us here had tried to lead me and Francette to another room at first, but Mariel insisted that we stay with her. When the guards argued that they couldn't agree to that, she turned on her heel and started to leave. The guards stopped her in a fluster, and she told them to report to the king that the guards had made her leave.

To be told that you're going to be held personally responsible is probably one's worst nightmare for anyone working at a public-facing job like this...

After Mariel had made her declaration right in the guard's face, he had glanced at his colleague...but the other guard stood several meters away, pretending he hadn't heard anything. It wasn't as if they could go to the king or minister to ask where they should take the maids. And if he was to ask his superior, he would just be told to figure it out himself.

...Because he didn't want to take responsibility for it either. Their superior could just claim his men did it without running it by him to avoid being held accountable, after all. He might be criticized a bit for not training his men well enough, but it was far better than taking the entirety of the blame on himself.

And what would happen if word reached the king that someone had decided to turn away the beloved child of the Goddess...? Yeah, he'd have quite the happy future waiting for him.

Chapter 39: Negotiations

So, in the end, the flustered guard ended up deciding to lead us into the room as if nothing had happened. He let us in so naturally that the other guard waiting in front of the room ignored us, too. And since the king had no idea any of this had happened, it seemed he figured there was some sort of reason we were here that the coordinators were already aware of, and therefore decided not to think about it too much.

Of course he did. Who would even imagine that a little noble girl would force the royal guards to let her maids into a meeting with the king?! In any case, the count and Mariel were motioned to take a seat, so they each sat down.

Francette and I stood behind Mariel, of course. Francette was probably thinking about how it would take a moment longer to draw her sword and cut down an opponent from a seated position.

...No, we aren't cutting the king down! We'd be wanted criminals...

The sword was in my Item Box, anyway.

"...What happened to your parents and your brother was truly tragic. They were great aristocrats, and such wonderful people..."

The king obviously didn't mean it, since Count Maslias had told us that the king had barely ever interacted with the late Viscount Raphael. They'd probably seen each other when Viscount Raphael first took over as head of the household and during important ceremonies, but it was questionable that the king even remembered the faces of the lower nobles. That said, Mariel surely didn't mind receiving those comments, even if she knew they were just flattery.

Mariel lowered her head quietly. They exchanged pleasantries for some time, then the king finally moved on to the main topic.

"Though you may be a young woman, your resolve to succeed your father, and to protect your domain and its people, is highly commendable... But is it not too heavy a burden for your shoulders?

I'd like to propose an idea. What do you say to me becoming your caretaker and protecting you from the rabble who mean you harm?"

Here we go...

But House Raphael, along with their parent household of House Maslias, were under the faction led by Marquis Cedric, which was separate from the royal family and the temple, more akin to a merchant faction.

...In other words, the king was trying to headhunt her right in front of the leader of the faction that House Raphael belonged to. Maybe he figured that Mariel was an innocent young girl who wouldn't question the authority of a king, and that she would leap at the opportunity to have such a powerful figure at her back. But we had expected this would happen.

Mariel replied, "I am incredibly grateful for your kind words, Your Majesty. ...However, I must humbly decline your offer. Count Maslias, whose household has been the parent house of House Raphael for generations, is already my caretaker..."

It was the obvious response. Mariel didn't owe Marquis Cedric anything, but there was no way she could have betrayed Count Maslias. The king didn't know much about the relationship between Mariel and Count Maslias, but maybe he was aware that she wouldn't turn her back on her parent house or faction so easily. The king, therefore, followed up with his next attack without hesitation.

"So, what do you say to marrying my son?"

...He wasn't even listening to Mariel's response... In fact, the king intended to ignore her intentions and push his own agenda through by force. He was looking down on her as nothing but a lower-class noble, and he was completely ignoring Cedric, who was a marquis, albeit a minor one.

Chapter 39: Negotiations

"Your Majesty, Viscountess Raphael has just recently lost her family, and..."

Even though it was the king he was speaking to, Marquis Cedric couldn't let such pushy and thoughtless behavior pass. However, when he chimed in, the king simply pretended the marquis didn't even exist. The king tried to go on, but...

"Your Majesty, I do believe your sons are the crown prince, who is forty-eight, and his brother, the second prince, who is forty-five? And as far as I'm aware, they are both married already... Is this an invitation to be a mistress, perhaps?" Mariel asked with a smile... But her smile didn't reach her eyes.

Yes, of course we had already done some digging into the king's relatives. I mean, a "prince" could be middle-aged, or even an old man if the king had lived long enough. It wasn't as if every prince was young and handsome. It stands to reason that some of them are bald guys with beer bellies...

Then I noticed Mariel's right pointer finger bending as if tugging on an invisible string.

Whoa, she's mad! I think I can see a vein popping in her temple... So, I guess we're doing this?

No, I didn't think explosions would be a good idea when dealing with the king. It could cause a *coup d'état* or something...

"This is a great offer, is it not? This way, you will be a member of the royal family and..."

Pang!

"Gaaah!"

The king lurched forward in pain, his minister and guard staring at him, frozen and speechless...

I mean, of course they'd react that way. A metal basin had just landed on the king's head out of nowhere...

We were indoors, so there was nothing but the ceiling above us. Just empty air. There was no way such a thing could have come falling down. That is, unless a goddess was involved...

Of course, I made sure to be very careful dropping this metal basin. They tended to be pretty hard and heavy. In those comedy sketches from way back when, the metal basins were made of aluminum or softer material, the person who was getting hit by them wore special wigs with a thin layer of metal in them, and intricate calculations were done when dropping them to ensure the angle would be just right, so there were all sorts of precautions in place. And then there's Celes, who just dropped that wooden bucket without putting much thought into it...

Yeah, I'm talking about that time when Layette was kidnapped!

So anyway, since we were dealing with an old man here, I made sure to use a metal basin made of super-thin aluminum, one that couldn't be used for its intended purpose due to its light weight and softness. There were a few drops of potion inside, which allowed me to conjure it as a "container."

Its appearance and the sound of its impact were pretty noticeable, but it shouldn't have hurt too much.

"Wha..."

The king stood there dumbfounded, staring at the metal basin as it clattered around on the ground.

Then...

"I-It disappeared!!!"

Yeah, I put it away into my Item Box. I didn't want it to become a target of their worship as the Holy Basin or something.

"..."

Then, after some time had passed in silence, Mariel unleashed her special move, the one that she had rehearsed so many times.

Chapter 39: Negotiations

"O Goddess, please wait a little while longer before choosing to destroy the royal palace after murdering the royal family and its ministers..." Mariel said, clasping her hands together and looking up at a thirty-degree angle into the sky as she uttered the prayer.

It was the same move she'd pulled at the count's place.

Then...

"Gyaaaaaa!!!"

Within the chaos, I glanced over to Marquis Cedric to see a serene smile upon his face. It seemed he had come to a realization... Or maybe it was the expression of a man who had simply given up, or decided to stop thinking...

But the chaos settled as abruptly as it had come, and the king and his ministers stood from their chairs and lowered their heads. I thought they might even end up rubbing their noses on the ground, but guess not...

"I-I apologize. Forgive my discourtesy... A-And, please, quell the Goddess's wrath on our behalf!"

It was unheard of for the king to lower his head to a mere viscountess, and an underage girl no less, but he was seeking forgiveness not from Mariel, but from the goddess at her back. So that was completely fine, then.

"Then you must never bring up talk of marriage before me ever again. You must never meddle in my affairs or say anything about me to my parent house or anyone else. And you must never get involved with House Raphael for any reason...oh, that is, unless it's about providing support, monetary or otherwise, upgrading my title, or other such beneficial topics..."

Whoa, Mariel just threw some off-script lines in there just now! She's got quite the nerve for someone with such a cute face...

As for the king, he nodded repeatedly like a broken toy, without even thinking of denying her...

All right, mission complete!

Some inoffensive conversation went on for some time after, then we dispersed.

The king and his men were frozen in fear at the idea that it could all be over with one poorly chosen comment. The tables had turned so drastically that it was hard to tell which side was the little girl's.

The worst part was the impish smile on Mariel's face as she made politically risque comments to provoke the king, knowing full well what was going on in his mind.

...You're scaring me here!

And so, the day ended without issue. Tomorrow was going to be the main event.

No, to Mariel, yesterday was the preliminary skirmish, today was the main event, and everything from tomorrow onward was nothing more than finishing up some unsettled business. But providing support for Mariel was nothing but a side mission for us. Our main objective was something else...

Yes, we were here to flush out the ones who had gone after Layette. And tomorrow, we were leaving Count Maslias's manor to stay at a fancy inn so we could do our own thing.

Now that Mariel had finished her round of greetings, led by Marquis Cedric, she would meet with other noble houses regardless of faction and get connected with the merchant houses in her capacity as the head of House Raphael rather than as the beloved child of the Goddess. It was too much to ask of the other parties to

Chapter 39: Negotiations

come by for those meetings while we were staying at Count Maslias's place, so we decided to move out.

And of course, they *all* came to visit.

Aristocrats from Mariel's faction. Aristocrats from other factions. Politicians. High-ranking military officers. Merchants. Priests. Speculators and swindlers. And people who seemed like normal people in public, but were actually the bosses of criminal organizations...

I had already expected that things would quickly get out of hand with influential people brute-forcing their way to arrange meetings as soon as we moved to the inn. That was why we stayed at Count Maslias's place, but surely word of the incidents at Count What's-His-Name's manor and at the royal palace had already spread. I had already informed various groups of the conditions and procedures for meeting with Mariel, so I had already narrowed down the selection of people hoping to see her. As such, I figured things wouldn't get too chaotic.

Those who had heard about "the Goddess's frustration" probably wouldn't say anything that crossed any lines, and those who were devout or already well-informed would know to watch their tongues.

But anyone who assumed Mariel was just a little girl taking advantage of sheer coincidence, or some average girl who had just so happened to be saved by the Goddess, or a naive child who could be taken advantage of with a little smooth talking...well, they might try making a move again. And that noble who tried to fake a crisis just to swoop in to the rescue would probably come, too.

And more importantly... I was almost certain that whoever had ordered the attack on Layette would contact us again. That was why, for us, this was the "main event"...

"Thank you for everything. I will be sure to repay your kindness one day..."

With that, Mariel and the rest of us left Count Maslias's manor. The count saw us off with a smile.

Even though he was spooked by the Mysterious Explosion at the Count's House Incident and the Mysterious Metal Basin at the Royal Palace Incident that he heard about from Marquis Cedric, he seemed to understand that Mariel herself was just an ordinary girl and that nothing bad would happen as long as you didn't try to force her to do something against her will. He had acted a bit awkward around Mariel for a bit, but he was now back to his usual grandfatherly demeanor.

Speaking of which, Marquis Cedric had maintained his serene expression after leaving the royal palace, as if he had been rid of a spirit possessing him. It seemed that he had returned to the relatively humble and gentle old man he was before, after giving up on his ambition of using Mariel to rise up in the world.

Word about the incident at the royal palace probably wouldn't spread too much, but the mysterious explosion at the count's house had to be known among the nobles within the faction at the very least. Some of them might try to ask for favors just because they were in the same faction as Mariel, but I doubted they'd try to get too aggressive.

As for the rest of the nobles, Mariel could work with those who would be useful to her and reject any who weren't. That was all up to Viscountess Mariel von Raphael, the head of House Raphael.

Our booking at the inn had been arranged by Count Maslias. It was a suite of five rooms, including a drawing room where we could hold meetings, so it suited our needs nicely. Two of the rooms were bedrooms; one of them was for the mistress and the other was for servants. Each bedroom came with four beds.

Chapter 39: Negotiations

Mariel, Layette, Francette, Belle, and I were staying in the mistress's room. Roland, Emile, and the two male servants from House Raphael were staying in the other. The female-only room was a bit over capacity, but Layette was sleeping in my bed, so it wasn't really a huge issue.

We had to split the guys and girls, since there was no way Francette would stay apart from me while in foreign territory, and there was no way I was gonna do without Layette... That left no other option. The rest of the servants were in other, cheaper rooms. It may have been a fancy inn, but there were still rooms for servants and guards, too.

We moved to the inn, rested, and had some meetings in the morning, then had some brunch and a siesta to prepare for the upcoming afternoon battle. They say you can't fight on an empty stomach, and that you should rest after a meal no matter what. There is meaning to any saying that has been passed down from olden times. You can't go wrong if you follow one.

I took a nice long rest after the meal, but since we had taken brunch pretty early, Mariel's meetings with the guests started first thing in the afternoon. The staff at the inn were already aware that we would be having many guests, since Count Maslias had made sure this was communicated upon booking the rooms. Since this was a high-end inn, many influential and famous people visited often, so they were used to this sort of thing. That was why they had a suite like ours in the first place.

According to the count, the inn's staff members had said that it was an honor to have the child of the Goddess stay at our inn and that we shouldn't hesitate to ask for anything, so they would surely side with us if some sort of argument broke out with a visitor. Even if that visitor was someone of high status.

Though, it was only natural for the inn to protect their paying guests, unless they were criminals or something. What kind of high-end inn would sell out their guests in the face of authority? And if they did anything like that to Mariel, I'd make sure they regretted it.

Anyway, our meetings with the guests had begun...

The first ones to pass through seemed to be from a noble family. Apparently, they had been in line since dawn. We had given out a prior notice that Mariel would be seeing visitors here from the afternoon onward. Some of the servants had been staying at this inn since arriving from the capital, so we probably could have started receiving them from early morning if we wanted, but...

"Bet the servants and the inn's staff weren't too happy about that..."

They were probably woken up from their sleep. Mariel had a forced smile on her face in reaction to my comment.

Well, that was part of their job, and that was probably the whole reason why they were staying at this inn with us in the first place. Maybe we were lucky that there weren't any people who had decided to wait here all night. I don't think I could have handled it if a bunch of people stayed here overnight, chatting it up and screaming with their friends to keep themselves entertained. Someone probably would have called the guards.

"But if they lined up that long, they're probably retainers rather than the aristocrats themselves."

Mariel was right; no aristocrat would bear such discomfort for so long. They probably had their retainer line up to deliver an invitation to their manor or some other message. Though, Mariel wasn't going to take up an offer like that.

Of course, we didn't allow people to swap places with someone else after lining up to see us. If we permitted that, a bunch of people would have just hired stand-ins to line up in their place. Anyone like that had no right to see the child of the Goddess. We had spelled it out plainly on the notice, too.

Inside the room, Mariel sat on the edge of an oval table with her retainers on either side. Roland was to their right, I was to their left, and Francette was to the left of me. This arrangement was the compromise Francette had suggested, so we could still protect Mariel while Francette could protect me. This way, even if the person sitting on the other side had a weapon, Francette and Roland could stop them for sure. This arrangement also allowed Mariel to see any signals given out by us, and by her retainers, who had done prior research on the capital's inhabitants.

Belle and Emile had Layette with them, and sat in chairs behind Mariel. They insisted on escorting me, too, and we couldn't just leave Layette by herself in foreign territory, so this was the result.

And the first one to enter the room was...

"It's a pleasure to make your acquaintance. I am Baron Dorivell."

The old man was a baron, and although Mariel was new to her title, she was a viscountess. Besides, he was the one who had asked to see Mariel, so she was obviously the one in a higher position here. But even then, it seemed hard to speak with such reverence to a girl that wasn't even of age yet...

Though, he was an aristocrat, so I'm sure he was able to put his personal feelings aside. There must have been times when he had spoken to a count who was younger than him, or even the son of a marquis.

...Wait, it wasn't his retainer who lined up after all?! The head of the noble house himself had been waiting here since before dawn! That was actually pretty impressive.

But why had he gone through all that to speak with Mariel...?

"Much like House Raphael, House Dorivell was saved by the Goddess. As someone who received the grace of the Goddess,

I humbly offer you my full support. Please don't hesitate to call for my aid, should you ever need it."

Huh? Wait a minute...

"I will never forget the day you saved my oldest son Challotte with the Goddess's medicine. My household will pass down the word for generations to come, and I vow that we will rally to the Goddess's call as her vanguard to the very end. My entire family line shall devote ourselves to you..."

...Wait, why did he just turn slightly to face me instead of Mariel? I had worn a mask back then, so he shouldn't know what my face looks like... But those words were obviously not meant for Mariel. That meant...

I gave him the faintest of nods. It was so slight that it seemed like my head just so happened to move a little bit unless you were paying attention.

The baron's face then broke out into a wide smile, then he bowed deeply...directly toward me.

He knows...

Oh well!

Chapter 39: Negotiations

"If Lady Mariel is ever in danger, please do come to her aid..." I said, playing the part of a ladies' maid...though no ladies' maid would dare butt into a conversation between her mistress and another aristocrat.

The baron nodded deeply again, then spoke to Mariel for a bit about practical matters before he left.

"Lady Kaoru, was that..." Mariel began to ask. She had addressed me as "Lady Kaoru," but since there was no one around besides her own retainers and servants, I let it slide.

"I cured his oldest son when he was ill. That's all."

"..."

The members of the Raphael household all looked at me with exasperation.

What did I say?

In any case, it was time for the next guest.

"I am Eridel of the Griffon Trading Company. It's a pleasure to meet you!"

"Ah..."

"Huh? Ah..."

Our eyes met, and we both froze. Yes, we knew each other. It was one of the four merchants from the capital who had gone to Convenience Store Belle to try to get ahead of his colleagues.

"Why are you here...?"

Don't ask me...

"I was hired by the viscountess to accompany her on her expedition to the capital. What of it?"

It wasn't as if this guy had authority over me, so I didn't care to be polite.

"..."

Eridel made an awkward expression, but it seemed he couldn't think of anything to say and ignored me to speak to Mariel.

"Thank you very much for your time today. We of the Griffon Trading Company..."

But two of her retainers and I were already sending hand signals.

"Untrustworthy."

"Untrustworthy."

"Untrustworthy."

Yup, my assessment matched with that of the two retainers.

Mariel nodded slightly, so she likely wouldn't promise this guy anything.

"...Good day, then..."

A few minutes later, Mariel had ignored all requests from Eridel and ended the meeting as quickly as possible, sending him off on his way with her magic spell that actually meant "Get the hell out of here already."

Eridel looked like he still wanted to talk, but it seemed he wasn't shameless enough to hang in there after being told so blatantly that the meeting was over. But maybe it had something to do with Francette being there, adorned in her knight's gear instead of her maid outfit, and lightly touching the hilt of her sword.

"Okay, next visitor!"

Then a middle-aged man dressed like a merchant entered the room.

"Ah."

"Ah."

...Right, the four merchants from back then were the heads of big-time merchant groups. It made sense that the others would take the same course of action as Eridel had. I mean, he had taken a long journey to visit the child of the Goddess, so there was no way he wouldn't try to see her when she had come to him... Of course.

Chapter 39: Negotiations

Afterward, we went through the rest of the four merchants, along with various other merchants and aristocrats. I mean, it wasn't as if all of those merchants were bad guys. Other than the one who tried to get ahead of the others and the one who had gotten violent, they were normal, mild-mannered but driven people who ventured out through danger to try to seize a chance to make some profit. And their information-gathering was top-notch, too.

So, Mariel talked to those two normally. Her two retainers also signaled that the two decent merchants were fine.

Mariel dealt with some visitors off-handedly, while making favorable connections and deals to change goods produced from each other's domains. As she interacted with aristocrats, merchants, and the priests that were added to the mix for some reason, "he" appeared.

Yes, the phony aristocrat who had stirred up fake trouble to paint himself as the hero. He wasn't from the same faction as House Raphael, but a slightly bigger one. Supposedly, it had connections to the Temple of the Goddess…

"Pleasure to meet you. I am Harold von Halarel. I have heard you are familiar with the Goddess, so why not connect with House Halarel, which has strong ties with the Temple of the Goddess, and receive her blessing together?"

Of course, I had already flashed the signal meaning, "This is the guy!"

And so…

"Are you sure you don't mean you have strong ties with bandits?"

Mariel hits him with a super fast pitch straight down the middle! Well, making small talk with the likes of him would have been a waste of time, anyway.

"Wha…"

I wasn't surprised to see his shock as the color drained from his face.

"Wh-What sort of baseless... Where's your proof?!"

He became aggressive so suddenly, even though he was talking to a little girl... He seemed rather flustered. But Mariel didn't seem to care.

"Proof? I heard it directly from the Goddess herself. What other proof do you need? And it's pointless trying to convince me of anything. After all, I already know the truth. You cannot fool me with your excuses, and your arguments will have no effect on me. I don't seek anything from you, and nothing you say will convince me that the words of the Goddess are lies and your words are truth. Therefore, you are the one who made the bandits attack us. It's not possible for you to change this fact. You must realize this, do you not?"

There was nothing he could say in rebuttal to Mariel's statements. There was no way Mariel would doubt me after I had directly told her the culprit's name, and the count was wasting his time trying to deny it. Besides, how could he deny the words of the Goddess when he was supposedly a supporter of the temple? Furthermore, Mariel had only pointed out that he was responsible for the bandit attack, and didn't touch on anything about the mounted soldiers he had prepared to "save" us from the bandits. So, as it was, it sounded as if the count had tried to orchestrate an actual attack on us.

But it wasn't as if he could say that he actually had soldiers ready to help us or something like that. That would have been equivalent to a confession that he'd set up the bandit attack. Though, if you ask me, admitting that he tried to set up the phony attack to get closer to Mariel but didn't intend to harm her in the first place was way better than being seen as someone who had tried to arrange

Chapter 39: Negotiations

an actual attack on her. We already knew about the whole bandit incident, after all...

The count was sweating pretty hard now. But hadn't he already gotten reports from his soldiers that Mariel was protected by dogs and birds, the servants of the Goddess...? If so, wouldn't it be natural to assume that the Eyes of the Goddess was still involved with Mariel? Why didn't he think of that possibility?

Could it be that he didn't believe Mariel was loved by the Goddess as they said? Did he assume that she was a fake, but still tried to get in contact with her to use her anyway? That would make sense, since he wouldn't have tried to deceive or challenge someone who was favored by the Goddess otherwise.

Before, I thought that maybe he wasn't so bad, considering he didn't intend to actually hurt Mariel...but come to think of it, he was an aristocrat who was chums with bandits...

Out! Yooou're outta theeere!

Of course he was a scoundrel! He must have done all sorts of scummy things using those bandits! What was I thinking...?

"I would understand if I had made a report and you were trying to talk your way out of it. But what good do you think your excuses will do when I know the truth? Now, if you don't wish for me to expose your deeds to the others, leave at once!"

It seemed the count just gave up upon seeing Mariel so clearly displeased, and he left without putting up any further argument. As for Mariel...

"I told him to leave if he didn't want me to expose him, but I never claimed I wouldn't expose him if he left... That man left because he didn't want me to expose him. That is all, and it has no effect on what I decide to do!"

Mhm, looks like Mariel has fallen to the dark side...

And after dealing with several other visitors...

Twitch!

Someone entered the room and reacted with surprise the moment he saw us. The surprise showed only for a moment, but in that moment his face had frozen up. I noticed that in that moment of frozen surprise, he was looking right at me.

"I am Dobul, the head of the Banshee Trading Company. Regarding the beloved child of the Goddess, Viscountess Raphael..."

Mariel dealt with this merchant lightly, as she had with many of the previous visitors.

He was more persistent than any of the others, and Mariel couldn't hide her displeasure in the end as she sent him home. I then told her, "Gimme a minute!" and leaped out of another door.

After that, I went outside through a side exit and raised my right hand... Then the one who had been waiting by this exit came flying right away... Literally.

I ran around the side of the inn and pointed at a certain man... It was the merchant from earlier, walking out of the front door and looking rather angry and frustrated.

Follow him!

Got it!

"It" affirmed my order, then flew into the sky in wide, circular motions. ...Of course, "it" was a member of the bird troops that served House Raphael.

I mean, I knew the merchant guy's name and the name of his business, but instead of using that information to find the location of his shop and residence, it was much easier to follow him. Someone might alert him or a guard if a stranger started snooping around...

So, for now, I decided to try to find out where this guy lived without asking for information from anyone else. I didn't bother putting on a disguise. It had been four years since I became known as the Angel of the Goddess and Celes descended upon the peace conference. I'm pretty sure there were a lot of people who had seen me or taken drawings of me to other countries since then. So, it wasn't too crazy to imagine that someone recognized me here, a country so far from the Kingdom of Balmore.

And if he decided not to say anything, pretending not to recognize me even though he clearly did... That made him very suspicious.

"I apologize for the wait!"

I quickly returned to the room and got back to the meetings. There were still many more visitors to see. And so, we got right back to it...

Twitch! Twitch! Twitch, twitch!

"...Huh?"

One after another, I started seeing more visitors react to seeing me by freezing for a moment, then acting as if nothing had happened.

What is going on?

Just then, Roland seemed to notice me thinking hard and muttered,

"...Are you sure they're not just getting scared by the look in your eyes?"

Damn it!!!

I made sure everyone who reacted to seeing me was tailed after they left. I had prepared plenty of troops for this purpose just in case.

Hahaha...

Actually, all of the bird troops had come with us and were just chilling in trees and roofs around here, anyway. They had come all the way here with us, so they weren't gonna pass up a chance to do something interesting or to earn special rewards.

But really, how can they be so smart?! You had a hand in this, didn't you, Celes?! Whatever you did to make them smarter, if you could give me some of that... No, no, I can't think about that!

Surely, there would be some sort of downside to going through such a thing. No, no, no, I wouldn't be me anymore. I would be a different person entirely. If I made my eyes cute and my breasts bigger using potions, that wouldn't be me anymore...

Hey, shut up!

"Do you think it's one of them, Kaoru?"

"Hnn..."

All I could do was groan in response to Francette's question.

I had Emile and Belle follow the birds to check the homes of each of the visitors who had reacted upon seeing me, but none of them were suspicious. Nothing much had happened since the meeting. If any of them knew about me, they surely would have made some sort of move by now... That must have meant the person I was looking for wasn't among Mariel's visitors this time.

It seemed it wasn't going to go so easily... But whoever it was had sent multiple people from the capital, so they were at least somewhat persistent.

They didn't try to make an aggressive move to get in contact with Mariel, who was an aristocrat and hard to get to, and they didn't try to make contact with me, even though I was living as a normal commoner. Instead, they had taken the extreme route of taking a hostage. It was hard to believe they would pass up such a perfect opportunity...

Ah.

"Was that everyone who asked to see Mariel?" I asked Mariel's retainer, the one who managed the appointments.

Chapter 39: Negotiations

"No, we accepted all meetings from noble houses, whether it was with the head of the house or their retainer in their stead. However, with the merchants, we turned down anyone who wasn't the head of the company themselves, or had a bad reputation, attitude, or manners. We also only accepted large trading companies, and turned down any smaller company unless they had an exceedingly good reputation... We would have had far too big of a list otherwise."

Ah, that made sense. Without rules like that, everyone would have made an appointment for the sake of it. We should have asked for a reservation fee. Not only would we have narrowed down the numbers, but we could have made some good money.

Come to think of it, even though all aristocratic types were let through, Mariel had acted coldly when it had been a retainer coming in instead of the aristocrat in question. It was only natural for her to react that way. If they thought sending a representative in their stead was good enough for this girl, of course they'd get the appropriate treatment back.

Maybe they had just been trying to send a retainer to invite Mariel to a dinner or a party, but she wasn't going to accept invitations from strangers to waste half of her day with them. And she couldn't bring guards or any of us to a dinner or a party, so she'd be in enemy territory all by herself. I couldn't let her go to such an event, not that Mariel herself had any intention of agreeing to something like that in the first place.

So, everyone who extended invitations by deliberately sending their retainers had bombed completely. It was pointless to negotiate with someone who wasn't even the head of the house, so Mariel just went through the pleasantries without talking about anything too specific, turned down all invitations, and had them leave pretty quickly.

The retainers had turned pale, desperately trying to salvage the conversation, but she had no obligation to keep it going. It didn't matter to her what rank the retainer's master was. It was impossible to accept invitations from literally every high-ranking noble, and she was simply turning down their invitations because her schedule didn't line up, so there was no one who could criticize her etiquette, either.

If they tried to make any accusations, the higher-ranking nobles from her faction should protect her. Especially considering she was a young and single young woman who was the head of a noble house, *and* the beloved child of the Goddess, the entire faction would have lent their collective strength to guard her. That was what factions were for in the first place, so they'd better…

So, there were no issues there. I was pretty sure of it.

Now, the problem was the merchants who hadn't gotten an appointment. If they wanted to get in contact with me or Mariel, they could have just used conventional means, assuming they were aristocrats or big-time merchants. Just like those four merchants from before. But instead, they went straight after someone who was connected to me.

That meant I was dealing with "those types."

Why didn't I realize it until now…?

"Do you have a list of people who were turned down?"

"Yes, of course. Such lists do tend to come in handy later on…"

Yeah, now *that's* a capable retainer.

Chapter 40: Bishop

Francette and I left the inn together and wandered around the capital. I wasn't wearing my maid outfit, but clothes that made me look somewhat wealthy. Francette was in her maid-looking outfit because it was easy to move around in rather than her knight's equipment, and carried her sword concealed in a tube-shaped container.

I didn't bother changing my hair color with potions or putting tape under my eyes to alter my appearance. I hadn't worn any disguises before now; if I suddenly started, the people from House Raphael might have let it slide, but the others would have found it odd. I had been hanging around Mariel for a while, so a lot of people probably recognized my face and hair color by now.

And the number one reason I wasn't wearing a disguise was because I wanted to settle this whole business already. We had already gotten Mariel's business out of the way, but Convenience Store Belle was still closed, and we didn't have access to fresh seafood like we did in that city.

…I mean, I did have a bunch of seafood in my Item Box, but it just wasn't the same. Besides, I was supposed to be Mariel's maid, so we couldn't use the inn's kitchen and start cooking dishes just for us.

So, that's why I wanted to get this all over with. Anyway, this was meant to be bait. Bait to bring out those who wanted to make an aggressive move against me, rather than Mariel…

If they were up to something, they'd probably have someone watching the entrance to the inn. That way, if they caught Mariel stepping out, they could make contact with her and act like it was just a coincidence. And if her servants stepped out, they could make contact and try to get information from them via bribes or threats. Of course, whoever was behind it would send one of their thugs in their place, to make sure their own name wasn't revealed.

That was why I dangled this bait out for whoever was on lookout. They would surely report that Mariel's maid was dressed in a most un-maidly fashion, and accompanied by a maid of her own. Anyone who knew me...or rather, "the Angel of Balmore," would definitely take the bait.

I had been thinking just that when someone approached me.

"Pardon me, may I speak to you for a moment?"

The person who spoke to me had to be around fifty or so. He was an overweight man and seemed far from the fighting type. He had a mild-mannered demeanor and looked most like the retired head of a merchant house, probably safely married.

But of course, I didn't let down my guard based on his appearance. Swindlers tend to *seem* honest, after all.

Francette was using her right hand to reach into the tube she was carrying... Yes, she was gripping the hilt of the sword concealed inside. I had no doubt that if the man suddenly pulled a blade out of his chest pocket, she would cut off both of his arms before he got it anywhere near me.

Francette knew this, so she wasn't particularly nervous or anything, but it was possible that he had some trick up his sleeve... He could have had a needle or poison mist concealed in his mouth,

Chapter 40: Bishop

or he might try to blow us up along with him with some explosives… There was a possibility that he had set up an ambush, too, so we couldn't let our guards down.

"You are?"

"My name is Goscal. I have been sent here at Bishop Bruce's request to act as a mediator with the Angel. I say 'mediator,' of course, but my role is simply to bring you Bishop Bruce for your meeting…"

Unexpectedly, I had been approached by the Temple of the Goddess rather than a merchant… But if he was making contact with me instead of Mariel, he either knew who I was or he wanted to gain favor with one of House Raphael's servants… Wait, what am I, stupid? This guy just called me "the Angel"… I need to get it together…

Well, it made sense that the temple would have more accurate information about the incident at Balmore than a merchant would. They were one of the involved parties, after all. They must have been directly contacted by the Temple of the Goddess in the Kingdom of Balmore. Their intel had to be far more accurate, considering merchants had to piece together vague rumors they got by word of mouth. Likewise, the royal palace seemed to be putting in an effort to gather accurate information, but the "accurate information" they'd been getting mainly consisted of rumors or official announcements that had been released by Balmore's royal palace, so their info was heavily manipulated…

So, anyway.

"Please lead the way, then."

Yep, of course I was gonna take the sketchy invitation. That was the whole point of putting out the bait…

"Thank you very much for coming. My name is Bruce, and I am a bishop."

The fat man Goscal led us to an inn that was pretty fancy, albeit a bit lower in status than the one we were staying at. I figured if a woman screamed in an inn of this level, it was highly unlikely to be ignored, regardless of whether or not that woman was a guest with a room here.

Though, if something was to happen, it would probably be them crying for help, not me. Francette could deal with any ambush with her superior reflexes, and I could use my Item Box and potion-creating abilities as long as I was given the time to act, so there was nothing we couldn't handle... Probably.

"I'm Kaoru. She's a maid... So, what business do you have with me?"

The fact that Francette and Roland were traveling with me had never been made public. Well, I guess the fact that I had left on a journey had never been made public, either. In any case, I couldn't mention Fearsome Fran here, considering her name was the second most well-known in Balmore, next to the name of the kingdom itself.

Me? I was known as the Angel, and the name "Kaoru" was far less known than Francette's. It wasn't like that bothered me or anything... No, really!

Anyway, I decided to introduce Francette as a normal maid who happened to be holding a dubious, tube-shaped object, and I only gave him my own name. This Bishop Bruce guy was after me, with no interest in some random maid, so this was no problem.

Just who was this bishop, and what was he after...?

"Pardon me for getting straight to the main topic. To tell you the truth, I am not from this country. I've come from the Kingdom of Brancott, and I am here on behalf of the royal palace there."

Chapter 40: Bishop

Wha...

Brancott, the kingdom where that stalker crown prince was from... The temple there was always clashing with their royal palace for power, just like this country and the Kingdom of Balmore, so there shouldn't have been such a thing as a priest working for the royal palace...

But I heard that the state of the Temple of the Goddess in each country had changed since the peace conference with Celes, so it wouldn't be surprising if the system wasn't how it used to be... I wanted nothing to do with this if it was related to that crown prince, but that didn't seem to be the case.

But I was surprised this guy had followed me this far. That stalker prince had long since given up, after all... So, what did he want?

"Well, regarding the king's heir, many have voiced their opinion that the wise Prince Ghislain is more deserving of the throne than your enemy, Prince Fernand. However, there are fools who support the useless and impudent Prince Fernand, spurring on dissidents, and we worry for the future of the kingdom..."

Oh, it was just some internal trouble... It might have been a big deal to those involved, but it didn't mean anything to anyone else. No matter who became king, it didn't really change things for farmers or foreigners... That is, unless that king was an absolute fool.

This had nothing to do with me, sure, but there was one thing that was annoying me. It seemed that I was being used as one of the reasons for this internal struggle.

True, that stalker prince had caused a lot of trouble for me. But it had been years since then, and according to the rumors, he was relatively respectable when it came to other matters, and it seemed like he wasn't that bad of a choice to be the next king. Comparatively, the second prince left something to be desired in terms of intelligence and personality. You could say he was the ideal target for disloyal retainers to take advantage of.

So, it seemed like they didn't want the prince using my name to take the throne... And yet, it looked like they assumed I'd side with the second prince, and wanted to use me because of what happened at the party at the royal palace and the way I had avoided the stalker since...

When I was in Balmore's royal capital, the second prince's people had kept trying to approach me, but I had turned them all down. In fact, I had told them the "Kaoru" who caused that incident at the party at Brancott's royal palace and the "Kaoru" known as the Angel of Balmore were two different people, Alfa and Mifa, so I didn't like how they just ignored that and tried to take advantage of me, assuming the two Kaorus were one and the same.

"And so, we would love for you to announce your official support for Prince Ghislain, Lady Angel..."

I had been staying silent, so the Bishop Bruce guy kept blabbing on. Did he even realize that he had presumed to mix up Alfa and Mifa? Lying to other people was one thing, but why was he spewing this nonsense to the very person it concerned?

Maybe he thought my explanation was a lie, or he didn't have accurate information? Hmm...

Either way, there was only one answer.

"I am not interested in the affairs of the human masses."

"Wha..."

Yeah, I've always had a policy not to discuss politics, religion, favorite baseball teams, or ramen. Those conversations never turned out well.

"Y-You...servant of the devil!!!"

Huh? Why had he flip-flopped so quickly? He snapped way too easily, don't you think? I was supposedly the messenger of the Goddess, right? Sure, he hadn't gotten the reply he was hoping for, but he went directly from asking nicely to calling me a servant of the devil? That was a bit extreme. Something was fishy. It was far too unnatural. It was like that's what he thought of me the entire time, and he'd accidentally let his thoughts slip out...

Come to think of it, that reminded me... There were some people who called me that long ago... Yes, they were priests of the religious nation now lost, Rueda.

"One of Rueda's, huh...?"

"H-How did you know?!"

Wow, what an idiot...

This guy was probably always on the deceiving side and had never experienced things the other way around. Not many would try to fool a priest in a world where the goddess actually existed, after all.

"You fled from Rueda, and now you're plotting to manipulate the idiot second son of Brancott. You never learn, do you...?"

"Wh-Why, you..."

The priest's anger reached a boiling point as I scoffed at him. It seemed he never had an ounce of reverence for me in the first place. Either he only intended to use me in the first place, or maybe he was planning on tricking me somehow, or he was actually plotting to find some opening to kill me so he wouldn't have to worry about me anymore...

"Whatever the case, diiiiiieeeeee!!!"

Fwsh!

Oh, so he was planning to kill me after all...

Maybe he had just decided to go on a whim right now, but considering he had a knife hidden in his chest pocket, it was probably pre-planned.

Chapter 40: Bishop

"Gyaaaaaa!!!"

The priest screamed, eyes bulging, as he stared at the severed wrists where his hands used to be. The hands in question could be found on the floor, one of which was still gripping the knife.

He was a total amateur; he had slowly pulled out a knife, pointed it at me, and charged. There was no way Francette would have let that pass without doing anything.

"Wh-What's the... Aaahhhhhh!!!"

By the time the inn's staff members came rushing in, Francette had already sheathed her sword and returned to being an ordinary maid holding a dubious-looking tube.

"It appears this thug has been struck with divine judgment. A priest who threatened a servant of the child of the Goddess and attacked when the servant refused to obey has been captured. Report as such to the royal palace, Temple of the Goddess, and the child of the Goddess. Quickly!"

"A-A-As you wish!"

Good, it seemed the situation was under control with my preemptive move to make sure they wouldn't cause a scene or try to have me arrested me. The priest was in no state to explain his side with all that pain, fear, despair, and confusion anyway. The best he could hope to do was scream and roll around until someone came to pick him up. Now, I was curious to see just how good the police in this country were at interrogation (torture).

Oh, and the fat person who had led us here was in the corner of the room, trembling on the floor. He was too scared of the look in Francette's eyes to even think of running away.

Good, Fran, you've mastered the Nagase-style Art of Glaring!

"...And that's what happened."

I had just finished explaining what happened to Mariel, Roland, the rest of our party, the royal guards from the palace, and the priests and paladins from the Temple of the Goddess. Then the royal guards and the priests started arguing about who was going to take the culprit into custody...

I mean, I didn't care who took him in as long as they told me the result of their interrogation. I'd instruct them through Mariel to make him blab about what he was plotting against the Angel, not just the child of the Goddess, so that should be covered, too.

If I didn't specifically tell them to do so, I probably wouldn't find out about his plans to use the servant (me) to harm the child of the Goddess. After all, it was likely that their plot had targeted me rather than Mariel...

It seemed their plan was to deceive and use me, and if that didn't work, eliminate me. But I didn't care about any of that. The question was whether or not they were the ones responsible for the attack on Layette. That was all I cared about right now.

In the end, the royal palace's people took the culprit into custody. I guess that was to be expected. The Temple of the Goddess had no legal authority in this case, and this could have ended up becoming a huge deal, so it wasn't something that could be left for the temple to handle. It wouldn't have surprised me if the king himself had said he wanted his people to handle this investigation.

I put the severed hands into my Item Box before the people from the temple and royal palace came by, and I used a potion to stop the hands from bleeding any further.

I also told the culprit, "Don't mention anything about me being the Angel. You will strictly refer to me as Mariel's maid when you testify. If you are remorseful and confess everything, I may consider reattaching your hands," so I figured things would probably work out.

It wouldn't be a big deal if he did end up blabbing about me, because I'd just move on to a new country. Just like that time I created a potion-dispensing mini Goddess statue and fled...

Honestly, I wanted to question him myself, but with the inn's staff and other patrons starting to gather around us and the fact that people from the royal palace and the Temple of the Goddess were likely to be here soon, it wasn't really possible at the moment. What a shame...

Well, I could just join the interrogation, what with my connection to the beloved child of the Goddess. I was a victim and directly involved in the incident, so if Mariel wished it, no one was going to stop me from attending the questioning of the one who meant her harm. If it came down to it, I could definitely get through by talking to the king directly.

Yeah, this "beloved child of the Goddess" thing was pretty convenient. I mean, I could do the same by using the Angel's name, but that would complicate things later on. The child of the Goddess could just feign ignorance and get away with anything, but the Angel would be swarmed with all sorts of requests.

Telling people that I wasn't the Angel was no use, so I had partially given up on that already. Maybe it wasn't catchy or clear enough, but Friend of the Goddess never did catch on... Damn it!

It turned out I didn't have to talk to the king after all. As a direct witness of the incident and the maidservant of Mariel, who was the target of the attack (or so we claimed), I was invited to the investigation along with Francette. This was strictly an investigation, and the real interrogation was to take place later in a room that was specifically for that purpose. I guess that wasn't the type of thing you should show a lady... In my mind, I had decided it was an interrogation. It could have actually been torture, but for my own mental well-being...

Anyway, I was surprised to find that the king himself was there. He probably wasn't getting directly involved with the investigation, but he couldn't just ignore the fact that the beloved child of the Goddess had been dragged into intrigue in his own country's capital. If something went wrong, it could have incurred the wrath of the Goddess. Yes, from the infamous Celes.

Of course he'd show up...

As the investigator asked various questions, I chimed in and asked some questions of my own. The investigator probably didn't like that, but he couldn't ask the right questions without all of the context. I was the only one who could ask about the attack on Layette that happened in Count Maslias's domain, or in other words, the city where Mariel's villa and my shop were located, as well as the situation in Brancott and details about the Rueda survivors. Besides, he answered with a sense of urgency whenever I asked a question, so it made the investigation go rather smoothly.

And so, the king let out a sigh of relief to find out his kingdom wasn't at fault, the investigator wondered what he was gonna do with the culprit, and we were deep in thought trying to figure out how to deal with this next...

"Guess it's about time for us to leave..." I said to everyone at the inn.

There may have been things I had to do, but I didn't need to be here at the capital for them. For now, the priority was to escort Mariel to her villa in Count Maslias's domain or to her residence in her own domain. The villa was probably safer. Afterward, I would

Chapter 40: Bishop

deal with the remnants of Rueda to make sure they wouldn't try anything funny again. That was the only option I had.

"What? Are we fleeing without doing anything?" Francette asked, as if shocked by how weak-spirited I was being.

"...Think about it. This isn't the enemy's home base. It's just their grunts here. Not to mention, we've already captured him to be dealt with. As such, we're not running away. We're pushing toward the enemy to attack!"

"Ah..." Francette's face broke into a smile.

How badly do you want to fight?!

According to the information that the priest had given us, after Rueda's corrupt priests had fallen apart, some of them had gathered their funds and converted them into gold, jewelry, and expensive art pieces, then left the country through Balmore and moved into the Kingdom of Brancott. After that, they moved farther to the east and split between those who fled to another country on the main continent and those who put down roots in Brancott as a means of plotting their return. Some of them turned their assets into cash to make their way in the financial world, some of them gave up their ambitions to live a life of leisure in hiding...and some of them planned to make a glorious return into the world of religion as a priest once again.

The ones who had left to go east or gone into hiding were fine. Whatever they had done in the past, I wasn't interested in doing anything to them. It wasn't as if I was a citizen of Rueda or the police. But those who were striving for glory in Brancott in the world of religion or finance... They were gonna be an issue.

If they had been honest and announced themselves as survivors of Rueda who had taken their money with them and escaped here, the marquis of the Rueda territories now within the kingdom of

Balmore would have sent out a team to arrest them and seize their funds. Brancott wouldn't want any trouble with the Kingdom of Balmore, or rather, the Goddess Celestine, so they would probably have handed them over without resistance.

So naturally, these guys kept their origins a secret and made up some lies about being high-ranking priests from a far-away country or sages that had been living in isolation until that point. Normally, no one would take them seriously...

Like I said, "normally." The massive fortune they had taken out of Rueda was enough to overturn any sense of normalcy.

One of the only two friends I had once told me the day after reading a manga that was purchased at a used book store...

"The world is all about money, zura!"

Chapter 41: Going Home

And so, we were quickly on our way back home.

The leader of House Raphael's faction, Marquis Cedric, the king, and the archbishop of the Temple of the Goddess all desperately tried to stop Mariel, but she responded saying that she didn't feel at peace staying in the capital where her maid had been attacked so blatantly. The king and the temple (especially the temple) couldn't say much to that, considering the attacker in question was a priest himself.

Not that they would have dared to be pushy with Mariel in the first place...

As for the priest who had tried to attack me, when I told him I might consider reattaching his hands, I did try to fulfill the promise... I only said I "might" consider it, and he was a bad guy, so I could have just ignored it. I didn't want to break any promises if I could avoid it, but I didn't have the time, since he got executed soon after.

I was surprised how quickly it happened, but since we got all the information we needed from him, this incident didn't have much to do with this country, and no one wanted to really get too deeply involved. Not to mention the Kingdom of Brancott and the Kingdom of Balmore would probably have demanded the priest's assets, so it seemed they put an end to him to avoid all that trouble.

Well, it was better to nip such troubles at the bud. Yup.

"What the?"

And so, we returned to our home sweet home, Convenience Store Belle, located in the capital of Count Maslias's domain. We had already seen Mariel and her crew off at House Raphael's estate in Count Maslias's domain. It was far safer than Mariel's home base in House Raphael's domain out in the countryside, and the location was much more convenient, with it being so close to Count Maslias. That was probably why her parents had always stayed there, instead.

Mariel's country manor could probably be completely destroyed by an attack from twenty to thirty bandits or so... Mariel had once told me that very thing before. So, it was probably best for her to stay here for some time. I doubted anyone would try something with the beloved child of the Goddess, but even if they didn't try anything blatant like a direct attack, it would be a pain in the ass for her if they begged her for help several nights in a row or something.

Anyway, that was fine and all. But...

What was this sketchy-looking piece of paper stuck on the shop's entrance?

"Contact me at once. £ ƒ § The Iron Saint"

I was able to read most of it, but it would've been impossible to decipher for anyone else...

Although, what kind of language was it if there were parts of it that even I couldn't read?

I was giving it some serious thought when Roland spoke up from behind.

"Ah, this is for me."

Huh?

"It's a secret code used by the royal family. It says, 'Contact me at once.'"

Yeah, I could read that part.

Chapter 41: Going Home

"What about after that?"

"That part says from £ to §, or from the royal guard to me. The symbols represent the sender and the intended recipient."

Ah, so since they were symbols, even a language master like me couldn't decipher them without knowing who they represented...

So what did this "Iron Saint" represent? Maybe I needed to understand the corresponding word to decipher that, too...

As I groaned and struggled to figure it out...

"'The Iron Saint' is just the name of the inn. The emissary must be staying there. Besides, that part is written in normal text, not in code."

...Damn it, I was overthinking it!

Anyway, it seemed this person had to urgently speak to Roland. They could have just checked in at the shop a couple times a day, but since they put this notice there out of sheer urgency, I decided to head to the Iron Saint inn instead of going back to the shop.

If I had gone inside and sat down, I wouldn't have wanted to move again for a few hours. All my stuff was inside the Item Box, so I figured it would be better to go straight to the inn. For a moment I debated whether I should leave Belle with Layette, but considering that this smelled like something that could be a pain to deal with, I didn't think Belle would just stay home without a fight.

Belle and Emile certainly were loyal to me, but that didn't mean they would do whatever I said. They would sometimes go against my orders if they thought it was for my own good. Though, they wouldn't ever disobey a firm order, as long as it wasn't unreasonable...

In other words, they wouldn't listen if I told them to leave me and run, or to prioritize their own lives over mine, but they didn't hesitate to obey the less important commands. Even if they put their own lives in danger.

I always told them not to act that way, but... I realized the other day that this tendency of theirs was a bad influence on Francette, so I had been re-educating them...

In any case, telling Belle to stay home right now would have been an unreasonable order in her mind. She would give her life to protect me, and considering I was heading into what could be trouble, it was only natural for her to try to approach the whole situation as my bodyguard.

Well, it didn't seem like I was in any immediate danger, and she could hear what happened from Emile later, so she probably would have backed down if I strongly insisted, but there was no need to go that far.

And so, we all headed toward the Iron Saint inn as a group.

"Sir Roland, it's so wonderful to see you again!"

It had only been a few months since he had left the kingdom, but the royal guard went down on one knee and lowered his head, getting overly emotional.

Well, he may not seem it, but Roland was the brother of the king, and he would have definitely become king if he hadn't gotten injured in that accident, so now that he was healed, people saw him as the person who should have been king.

His younger brother, the current king, was a good person, and Roland himself wished for his brother to remain on the throne, so it was a rather peaceful kingdom, without any power struggles within the family or worries about assassinations by disloyal retainers.

...Considering his status and position, maybe I had been treating him pretty badly? Oh well. In my view, he was just a pesky bug that had followed me on my journey against my will. In fact, he was a traitorous insect and a spy for the enemy, plotting to sabotage my important mission to find a marriage partner! He deserved whatever treatment he got!

"Yes, well done coming here. Are you alone?"

"Sir! There are two others in the capital, and we sent one more to the east, just in case!"

Roland had told me he was keeping his family up to date with letters. He must have been sending reports on our movements through those. So when the emissary arrived in town and found that we were away and the shop hadn't been abandoned, he probably asked around, then quickly found out about the miracle of the Bird Aristocrat and how we had headed for the capital. Considering the time frame in which we temporarily closed the shop and all the other factors, it would have been easy to figure out that we all went to the capital together... Unless he was an idiot, that is.

A member of the elite royal guard, and the one who was tasked with the most important role, no less, couldn't have been an idiot.

"What happened to those four?" I asked as the question came to mind.

Four royal guards had been sent to find us. Since we were talking about four royal guards, I was reminded of those four: *Those* royal guards, who I had granted one each of the Divine Sword Exhrotti after repelling the western Aligot Empire forces. Shouldn't they have come here? Roland had appointed them as his personal knights, after all. But this emissary wasn't one of them. That probably meant the other three were likely different people from the royal guards I knew.

The emissary understood my rather vague question and replied.

"The Four Walls are out securing the eastern border, my lady!"

"The Four Walls" was obviously referring to those four royal guards. The name was likely supposed to mean they were the four walls protecting the kingdom. The emissary knew me, so he answered in the same respectful tone he gave to Roland. But his reply did make me wonder...

"Securing the border? On the east side? But to the east are Brancott and Balmore, which are your two closest allies. And why were all four of them sent to secure that side of the kingdom?"

"That...is what I was about to explain..." he said with his brow wrinkled a bit.

Ah... It was one of those "I was just about to!" moments... My bad. Please go on and explain...

"There has been a political change in the neighboring kingdom of Brancott. We have reports that the second prince's faction has taken over the royal capital, and the first prince is said to have escaped the capital, but this has not yet been confirmed. And the second prince, who has become the provisional ruler..."

Yup, I knew what was coming. A classic move!

"He's making a move to declare war against other countries as a means to search for the first prince and control the military and the public sentiment, right?"

Chapter 41: Going Home

"Indeed. You are quick to catch on, Lady Angel..."

I thought so...

This was the most basic of classic moves! I'd seen it so many times that it was straight out of a TV drama playing at 20:45. They might as well start pulling out *inrō* pillboxes or bringing the Edo legal system into it.

"I have a message from His Majesty, Sir Roland. For the sake of confidentiality, I was ordered to relay it to you directly rather than via a written message. Here it is... 'Please come home, Big Brother~!!!' ...That is all."

What the heck?!

Ah, Roland's got his face down on the table... He didn't have to look so disappointed...

"Now, now, no need to make that face..."

Roland hung his head from his brother's unexpectedly pathetic message. I mean, they were so close, and he was a cute younger brother relying on his big bro, so I thought he should let it slide. My younger sister Yuki had relied on me for all sorts of things, and I did the same to my older brother. It was nothing to be ashamed of. It was proof of their close bond.

175

Kaoru's Younger Sister
Just her design was done during Volume 1...

Oh... Maybe he didn't mind it as a brother, but it was unbecoming of a king? I guess I couldn't blame him, then...

"...So, what are you gonna do?"

I actually already knew what Roland would do. He was the brother of the king, after all, and his home country, brother, retainers, and his people were in danger. If he didn't go back to help them now, I didn't want him in my party. I was more concerned about what Francette would say. Would she go back with Roland, or continue on my journey with me?

"Lady Kaoru, I must ask to have some time away," Francette said, naturally and without a hint of hesitation.

Well, that was the only correct thing to say there. Francette was Roland's betrothed, an aristocrat of the kingdom...and a knight. There was nothing else she could have said. Roland nodded with that same natural look, as if he knew she was going to say those exact words. ...Yeah, I knew. Of course I knew that was the kind of person Francette was...

Chapter 41: Going Home

And so...

"...Then I'll go to the realtor and stable to cancel the contracts. It's okay to clear out the shop tomorrow, right? And can you handle the business side of things yourself, Kaoru?"

"Yeah, sure. Tell them they can keep this month's payment."

"Got it!"

With that, Emile was off. Belle, who was holding Layette in her arms, looked as if she expected this, too.

They all understood so well.

"Huh?"

...Except those two.

"Listen, the orphans under my protection, the people who took care of me, people that I took care of, and many of my acquaintances are living in the capital. And whoever was working with that rotten priest who ordered the attack on Layette is on the enemy's side."

Yes, the "enemy"... The so-called second prince that had been set on a pedestal may have been told that I was his ally, supporting his bid for the throne, but screw that. They were all my enemies!

"And..."

"And?"

"They used me as a tool for their plot to seize the throne... Did you think I would let them go when they fabricated an oracle from the Goddess and spread their twisted message for their own personal gain?" I responded to Roland and Francette's simultaneous response with anger boiling in my voice.

Roland and Francette went down their knees and lowered their heads. The emissary did the same. Yes, it was time for a temporary return home.

Chapter 41: Going Home

"Finally, my time to shine!"

It was time for Ed to work for the first time in a while.

"We need to get back to the country where we lived before we left for this journey, stat! Can you do it?"

"Of course!!!" the five reliable voices replied in unison, and we were off.

I was gonna bring out the chariot after we got some distance from the city. So, for now, I held Layette in my arms as I rode Ed.

We had already finished paying off our balance at the stable.

"Okay, let's go!"

In dire cases when we really had to hurry…like when the children at the orphanage were in danger…I would do anything, without holding back. I would zip across the ocean in a high-speed cruiser, no, a jetfoil, or even fly there on a VTOL craft or helicopter, or even use a flying boat, or speed through the streets in a land cruiser…

But those methods would definitely cause a scene, and while I could produce ships and flying crafts as "potion containers," we still needed someone to pilot them safely. I may be able to drive something like a land cruiser because I had a driver's license, but not only would it cause chaos, but someone would probably stop us and take us in for questioning.

It'd be over if someone blocked the path with a carriage or log, and there would be times when we would have to stop due to conditions on the road, coming across a bridge, or running into other carriages. We would still need to rest, too. If we were ever surrounded, I couldn't just run over innocent soldiers to keep going…

Yeah, those methods shouldn't be used unless it really was an absolute emergency where every second counted.

And so, we took the normal route of riding on Ed and the other horses. With their potion-enhanced power, we didn't need to waste time stopping at inns, and could get there very quickly.

"…But I wonder why they decided to attack our Kingdom of Balmore when we have the Angel. Sure, you may be away temporarily, but it seems insane that anyone would think of making a move on your home territory…" Francette said during our meal-time break, and I couldn't blame her for wondering.

"They probably thought the Angel had abandoned Balmore, or that Balmore had lost the blessing of the Goddess. And since I rejected the first prince of Brancott, they likely assumed I would support the idea that the second prince should take the throne. Pretty presumptuous, or maybe someone filled their heads with such ideas… Seems like they think the Goddess is on their side. Must have bought into someone's nonsense…"

Chapter 41: Going Home

"Oh, I see..." Francette said, accepting my explanation right away.

According to Roland, the countries to the east of the Kingdom of Brancott, Drisard and the Kingdom of Jusral, were not only big countries themselves, but there were powerful countries positioned to their rear toward the mainland, so they weren't to be trifled with. So, this war to distract from the usurpation had to be with either the Kingdom of Balmore or the Kingdom of Aseed to the west. And Balmore had supposedly been abandoned by the Angel and forsaken by the Goddess, so it was an easy target to declare war on.

Well, an official declaration of war or actual fighting hadn't broken out yet, but according to the spies and plants in-country who had been feeding us reports, those details were pretty much accurate. Their target would probably only be one country. It was highly unlikely for them to wage a two-front war here.

What they didn't know was that the Kingdom of Balmore had formed a secret alliance with Aseed, as the country to their south that also shared a border with Balmore. So, whichever they decided to invade, the other would automatically join the fray. This alliance had actually been formed in preparation to deal with the Aligot Empire, and the two countries had come to that agreement in top-secret meetings after the previous peace conference.

One may think their alliance wouldn't work as a deterrent against attacks unless publicly announced, but the purpose was to deliver a fatal blow to attackers with an unexpected attack rather than to deter them. And announcing their alliance could have put the other countries on alert, supposedly...

Well, I didn't really understand politics. I decided to stay out of it. That is, except when it would be to my advantage.

And so, we began our advance once again. Considering we had a carriage drawn by a single horse, we were going at a ridiculous pace. Well, it was Ed's crew, after all. And they were all doped up with my potions.

So, we were traveling separately from the royal guards. We would have had to match their pace if they were with us, which would have slowed us down significantly. Even if Roland sent them back before us to deliver the news of our return, we definitely would have gotten there first.

So instead, he had the emissary stay in the city to inform the other three that their mission was complete. "Take it easy!" as they say.

And so, we continued at our own pace. We would dash through Brancott first, then into our old home of Balmore.

After that?

...Behold the wrath of the Nagase Clan!!!

...And so, here we are. The Kingdom of Brancott... Yup, this was the place where pictures...no, *wanted posters* of me had been passed around. Not to mention, this was a stalker nation, one that had sent their highest-ranking guards to the Kingdom of Balmore just to take a look at me, all so they could remember what I looked like.

They're stalking me on a nation-wide scale!

...And so, we came up with a plan. We had the ability to learn, after all!

"So, we will be splitting into teams. Roland and Francette will be Team Kobold. Everyone will be Team Horn Rabbit!"

"..."

The other five stared at me with a look that said, "There she goes starting something weird again..."

Chapter 41: Going Home

"The enemy is probably checking travelers based on the number of people we had in our group the last time we passed through, so we're gonna throw them off. I'll also be wearing a disguise. Layette wasn't with us last time, and by splitting our party in two, our composition will be completely different."

Two aristocratic-looking knights... They could be brother and sister, colleagues on the same mission, or lovers who had run off. Whatever the case, it wasn't a particularly strange combination, and it certainly wasn't weird enough that a border guard would investigate. In fact, a guard would be risking his head if he did... Not in the figurative sense, but literally.

Then there was the group of four commoners. Three of those were underage girls. A guard wouldn't be cautious of such a group. If anything, he'd worry about them. Three sisters traveling by horse but unable to find a carriage... And the older brother who seemed to be a fledgling hunter as their only guard, as unreliable as he seemed. There was nothing unnatural about it. It was just a run-of-the-mill kind of group that could be seen tens or hundreds of times a day.

They had thought Roland and Francette were my bodyguards the last time they saw me, so now that they wouldn't be with me. It was highly unlikely they would think I was the Angel. And with my disguise added to the mix... I would become the perfect mother. The other four seemed to understand after I gave my explanation. Layette still didn't seem to get it, but she didn't count.

And so, I wore my disguise to the border checkpoint and we split into two groups. Just in case things went south somehow, Team Kobold, consisting of Roland and Francette, made sure there were only two or three groups between them and the rest of us, also known as Team Horn Rabbit.

If we had gone first, Team Kobold would have had to run through the border checkpoint without going through their inspection, which would have been a huge deal. With us being in the back, they would only need to come back to us after their inspection was done, allowing them to avoid the serious crime of breaking through a border checkpoint by force. It may seem like a minor detail, but it made a huge difference.

Now, it's time to go to the border checkpoint!

...We got through without incident.

Yeah, I thought so.

Of course, I had put the chariot back in my Item Box, and I was riding Ed with Layette in my arms in front of me. As such, we were all considered normal riders carrying light personal items. Since we weren't bringing in any goods to sell, they weren't gonna tax us or anything. We basically got a free pass, and they just hurried us on through.

This was all thanks to my superior ability to disguise myself, of course. I changed the color of my hair and eyes. I also used invisible tape, adhesive, and Foundation...I mean, foundation...to make my eyes droopy. Though, if we're talking about the rise and fall of a nation, I guess Foundation works too. The words sound the same, anyway.

My hair and eye colors were one thing, but by making my eyes droopy, I had changed my appearance in a way that was directly at odds with my raison d'être, allowing me to avoid suspicion completely. This was the core part of what made me "me" as a human being, and the ultimate part of my existence that allowed everyone to recognize me...hey, shut up!

In any case, we entered the Kingdom of Brancott without any apparent suspicion.

Chapter 41: Going Home

"...I'm surprised we got through without being questioned..."

"Huh?"

Emile had made this comment suddenly, out of the blue.

"Why? There was nothing suspicious about us, was there?"

"A normal commoner child wouldn't be able to ride a horse, nor would they have the money to ride a horse bus, but we had three whole horses... We were definitely suspicious."

...

"You should have said so before we went in there!!!"

If he had given me a heads up, I could have prepared some sort of excuse! I mean, even if I had thought of one, we had ended up getting through without being questioned, so it would have been a waste of effort, but still...

"Next time, be sure to mention it if you notice something! Got it?"

"R-Right..."

He probably thought my plan was foolproof just because I had thought of it, and that it would have been rude to question me. That's no good. No good at all. I had to educate him some more...

After crossing the border, we regrouped with Team Kobold right away. Now we just had to split up when entering cities and when leaving the country. Or if we ran into any dubious-looking groups of soldiers...

If we caught sight of one from afar, both teams could make some space between us naturally and act as if we were separate groups. Inside the city, we could check in to the same inn separately and gather at one of our rooms later on. Though, really, we would mostly be camping, and we were only going to stay at an inn once every few days or so.

Of course, we could move a lot faster by doing the camping-only route. That could shave off a lot of wasted time. Even if it got a little dark, we could use chemical lights to illuminate our path. There might not be asphalt to walk over, but there shouldn't be any issues as long as we traveled over a decently-kept main road.

But with two-thirds of our members being female, we couldn't stand going without a bath at least once every couple of days. Even I had this desire, so it was probably even worse for Francette and Belle, who were with their respective loved ones.

When I said as such to Francette and Belle...

"What? No, not really..."

"I haven't really given that any thought..."

Y-You two... I-Is that how it is for other people?

Maybe it had to do with their historical backgrounds, our cultures, or even our natural dispositions... W-Well, maybe things were different here compared to Japan, where it was normal even for commoners to take baths since olden times...

But I couldn't stand not bathing, so we were staying at an inn with a bath once every few days! But, well, until then, we were going to camp out for now. And we would avoid the royal capital, instead passing through the south and thus into the Kingdom of Balmore...

"We're staying at an inn tonight. Then we head for the capital, Aras."

"Whyyyyyy?!"

Haah... Haah...

"Why would we go out of our way into a place where we'd be very likely to get recognized?!" I couldn't help but yell at Roland in response to his ridiculous comment.

What was he thinking?! Was he an idiot or something...?

Chapter 41: Going Home

"No, thinking ahead, it would be best to check on how things are in Brancott and gather what information we can as we pass through. No one was expecting you to return, so I don't think the risk is too great, either..."

Hmm... Roland did have a point too. But...

"Instead of us amateurs taking a huge risk in getting exposed, we've been getting intel from spies, plants, and lower aristocrats that have been paid off, right? That royal guard knows the first prince, so we already have a source of info, don't we? What need is there for us to go to the royal capital in person? Give me a reason besides a self-serving one!"

"Urgh..."

He's actually at a loss for words!

That meant he just wanted to go because he felt like it. That little...

Aaand we made it to Grua, the royal capital of the Kingdom of Balmore! ...The capital of Brancott? Like hell we're going there! We took a vote. It was five versus one. A landslide.

Francette, who could never agree with putting Roland and I in danger... Emile and Belle, who have sworn me their undying fealty... And Layette, who didn't understand what was going on, but was on my side anyway... There was no way I'd lose in a popularity contest.

And so, while ignoring Roland's rueful expression, we took a route far to the south to avoid Brancott's capital and safely arrived in Balmore's capital. Going back home and asking the king for the latest information was far quicker and more accurate than bumbling around trying to gather intel in Brancott. And hadn't we gotten a message from the king asking him to hurry back?! Even though he was Roland's younger brother, he was still the king, so he should follow his little brother's instructions...or rather, his command...

So, we arrived at the nostalgic capital, Grua. This place, the Kingdom of Balmore, was home to everyone besides Layette and myself. Even for someone who didn't have a homeland in this world, like me, well...it was the closest thing I had.

I had arrived in this world in the Kingdom of Brancott, and although I had stayed there for a while at first, I couldn't bring myself to call that place my homeland. If I did, the people from there would get carried away, and who knows what kind of nonsense they would start saying then.

Anyway, we began heading for the royal palace. If we went to the palace, we would get something to eat... I mean, we needed to gather information first and foremost, as well as check to see if there was anything urgent to take care of.

Of course, I had stashed the chariot back in my Item Box and had taken off my disguise since crossing the border and entering Balmore. There was no need to be in disguise here, and there was no need to put my chariot out on display, either. I was known throughout this kingdom, so as soon as people saw that I was the owner of the chariot, they'd start bothering me or bombarding me with requests.

Chapter 41: Going Home

That stuff was annoying, to be honest. I couldn't just punch them in the face or blow them up for coming at me with requests or invites, which made them all the more troublesome to deal with. They didn't give up after a rejection or two, either. I actually would have preferred that they attack me instead. Then I could crush them and be done with it... But no one in this country would try such a thing.

Actually...who knew how things were now? I wouldn't be surprised if Rueda survivors or spies...no, maybe even assassins from Brancott were lurking around. That Bishop Bruce guy who had tried to manipulate me and then immediately turned to kill me when that didn't work...

That guy's attitude had done a complete one-eighty far too quickly. The thought of killing the Angel had to have been brewing in his mind even before we met. It was likely that he already had a pre-set plan to talk me into doing what he wanted, and if that failed, he was just going to try to kill me... Actually, he was probably just following orders for the first part, but actually wanted to kill me the entire time.

I had a feeling they thought of me as a fiend, an enemy of the Goddess, a heretic, and a servant of the devil, someone who had brought ruin to Rueda...or more like ruin to everyone in Rueda involved with religion. But no matter how you looked at it, it was Celes herself who had dealt the finishing blow... A religious group, ended by the hand of the Goddess they worshiped.

Yeah, nope. I had never heard of anything like it before.

Well, it wasn't like they could go kill the Goddess herself, so I guess they had to direct their hate toward me. The attack that had made me go on a journey in the first place was caused by a single rotten priest from Rueda too. It was unlikely that that priest was the last one of those critters.

I mean, that Bruce guy had already admitted clearly that there were many others who had gotten out alive. And, supposedly, there were several who had taken part of Rueda's massive treasury with them, providing them with enough dry powder for all sorts of schemes.

Well, it was probably better to think about this stuff after talking to the king. I was about to get the latest info soon enough, so it was pointless to think it over now. My head had been tilted downward and staring around Roland's feet until now, but I looked up as I processed that thought. You gotta look up with your back straight and walk with confidence when going down the street… wait, what?!

"Whoa!"

A massive crowd had gathered to either side of the street, everyone happily waving their hands at me. Then…

"Hurrah for the Lady Angel! Hurrah for Lady Fran! Hurrah for Sir Roland!!!"

…I guess that was to be expected. The Angel of the Goddess, the great hero of the kingdom, and the brother of the king were all marching in together. Not to mention, the Angel had returned for the first time in months. Their fervor was understandable.

And now that I had appeared, well, you know. There were gonna be expectations for the return of my potions. The ones for sale, and the Goddess's mercy, in the form of the Tears of the Goddess…

No, the Tears of the Goddess were one thing, but I didn't have any intention of putting my potions up for sale again. Those things were a devil drug, something that would halt the progress of medical science and medicine, putting an end to doctors and apothecaries completely. They weren't something I should bring back. What if a

Chapter 41: Going Home

huge supply of them started going around, but then I wasn't around fifty years later or something? It would be an absolute catastrophe.

Me being absent would be one thing, but what if I was still here, but potions weren't being distributed anymore? Humans could never relinquish a luxury they have grown accustomed to. It probably would be for the best for me to leave this country again once I was done with my business. If I stuck around, the orphans of the Eyes of the Goddess would never leave me alone...I mean, leave the nest and become independent in their own right.

Maybe this was some sort of curse to bind me...

"Kaoru, we're here!"

"Oh... R-Right."

No good, I was zoning out with my thoughts and hadn't realized we were already in the king's office. There was no way we were going to be sent to the audience room, given the members of our party.

"Pardon us!"

Roland knocked lightly and opened the door. He pushed it open without waiting for a response, but that wasn't an issue here. This wasn't a place where the king would be conducting private affairs, after all. And even though they were related, here, they were just a guy and his older brother. It was standard for Roland to speak to the king with deference in public. They could go back to treating each other like brothers when they were alone or among their inner circle, but that would not fly out in the corridor where others could see.

"I'm so glad you're back, Brother!"

And the moment we closed the door behind us, Roland's brother Serge burst into tears and hugged him. He wasn't incompetent by any means, but he had always gotten support from his capable brother

Roland whenever he needed it. With the threat of war looming in Roland's absence, Serge must have been quite worried.

Well, he would probably fulfill his duty as king adequately enough if a war did break out, but having his brother by his side would make a huge difference.

Back when I was a student, I was also often asked by my classmates and underclassmen to accompany them when breaking up with the guys they were seeing. Supposedly, just having me there scared whoever they were breaking up with, so they didn't have to deal with any threats or persistent demands.

That's why I was known as the Master of Breakups. Everyone said, "If you're gonna break up with a guy, ask Nagase, the specialist in the field!"

...Shut up! Not once have I broken up with a guy myself!

How am I supposed to break up with someone when I've never dated anyone before, damn it?! Haah... Haah...

Anyway, we would hear what King Serge had to say, then decide how to deal with this from there. Or "who" to deal with...

Hurting Layette and the orphan children... Using my name as one of their excuses to usurp the throne... Trying to deceive and manipulate me, then trying to kill me when that failed...

Did they think I would let all that slide without doing anything? Even though there was no telling when they might hurt my loved ones again if left unchecked? Even though it would spread the idea that nothing would happen to anyone who messed with us? The pheasant would not be shot but for its cries...

Wait, why was His Majesty the King backing away with that tense look on his face? Yeah, one of my two friends had often told me, "Don't ever smile when children are around."

Chapter 41: Going Home

...Shaddap!!! ...Wait, oh!

We were in the royal palace, weren't we? Didn't I say that one time that I swore to Celes I would never set foot in the palace again? Oh no, I was thinking too hard on the walk here and completely forgot about that backstory... Not only did I waltz on into the royal palace, but I was all the way in the king's office! This was bad, I had to come up with some sort of excuse...

Extra Story: Mariel's Resolve

Lady Kaoru has left...

But there was nothing that could be done to prevent this. She has fulfilled her duty here and departed to take on her next task to destroy the enemies of the Goddess. I could never attempt to make Lady Kaoru stay here just for my sake when she was on her way to save so many others. She was the one who had saved me from being deceived into marrying my uncle Aragorn after he murdered my family, after all.

Lady Kaoru is a Goddess herself, not an Angel, as the world believes, and the only ones who know of this fact, other than her five companions, were my household and Baron Dorivell, who seemed to be somewhat aware of it after being saved by her, though he hasn't said so in any official capacity.

Not only did she save me at the cost of revealing such an important secret, she once again saved me when those with power sought to put me on a pedestal as the beloved child of the Goddess and take advantage of me. Even though I should have handled these incidents personally...

Normally, the Goddess will only bring salvation once. Once the Goddess departs after helping someone, it's up to them to seize happiness. But I... I am still able to continue using this ability to talk to animals.

...I won! No, that wasn't right. This wasn't about winning or losing.

In any case, my position and safety were secured thanks to the precautions Lady Kaoru had taken afterward. Those who heard about a "little incident" at a certain count's household and in the royal palace wouldn't dare demand I provide proof of being the beloved child of the Goddess. Those events may have been concealed from the common people, but they were well known among aristocrats and royalty. After all, since there was a possibility that one idiot's folly could destroy the entire country, it would have been pointless to worry about the king losing face.

And everyone would surely think that the Goddess's power is not something one should seek to use, but rather is something to avoid in order to prevent one's own ruin. That certainly wasn't incorrect. Lady Kaoru has clearly said she would show no mercy to anyone who means her or her loved ones harm...and she said to me, "Of course, you're one of those people who are dear to me, Mariel!"

Kyaaaaaa~!!! Haah... Haah...

But setting that aside. The Goddess of this world is, of course, Lady Celestine. She is our protector and has warned us of great catastrophes and defended us from impurities. ...She may not be one who minds the details, and doesn't seem to think too much about each individual human, b-but she can be considered a benevolent goddess. Yes, I think so...

But Lady Kaoru, a Goddess who descended to this world from another realm, has shown her mercy and brought salvation to a lowly girl like me, even though I surely must have looked like a pathetic wretch among lower beings. The Goddess of this world, Lady Celestine, sometimes saved humans on a whim, but was completely uninterested in individual humans, so at times, she would mass murde— I mean, deal with them somewhat harshly.

Comparatively, Lady Kaoru reaches out her hand to those who struggle as living creatures desperately trying to survive. Since I was no divinity but a mere human girl, I wished to— no, had to become bold and benevolent like Lady Kaoru, so I could at least protect and love those around me, such as my retainers and residents of my domain. This was my duty and my own way to express gratitude as someone who was saved by the Goddess.

Yes, I will be just like Lady Kaoru!

And just like Lady Kaoru, I would have a little girl like Layette, a gallant young woman like Lady Francette, and a handsome gentleman like Sir Roland serving me...

...Hehe. Hehehe. Heheheheh...

"My lady..." The butler spoke with a frown, eyebrows furrowed.

This butler was a trustworthy man who had served my family since my father's generation. He was a truly loyal retainer who didn't fear saying difficult things or giving words of caution out of fear of upsetting his master. And whenever he spoke with that expression, he was always about to mention something that was difficult to say. I had to make sure to listen well.

"Yes, what is it?"

The butler pieced together his words carefully as if truly struggling to get them out.

"...Has the look in your eyes gotten harsher as of late, my lady?"

What? Huh? Whaaat?

"G..."

"'G,' my lady?"

"Gyaaaaaaaaagh!!!"

I...I didn't want to be like her in *that* regard!!!

Extra Story: Mariel's Resolve

I-In any case, the Goddess of the other world, Lady Kaoru, had given me her favor and the ability to speak to animals, and I would use it to protect and advance my people and domain to live up to her expectations! In order to do that, I would overcome, crush, and trample any hardship or ordeal…

I'll do it! I, Mariel, will surely see it through!

So that one day, when I see Lady Kaoru again, I can stand tall and proud. Whether that will be in this world or the heavenly realm where goddesses reside…

Extra Story: Farewell Black Ops!

"We are destroying the Black Ops."

"What...?"

The old butler looked shocked by Mariel's sudden statement. He had served this household since the previous generation and had sworn his absolute loyalty to Mariel. That was exactly why he worried for her safety and was determined to stop her from undertaking such a dangerous course of action.

And now, at this moment! Out of his desire to repay the kindness the previous head of the house had given him, he would stop the young mistress even if he had to put his own life on the line! As he resolved to do just that...

"Of course, I will have someone else take care of it, so I won't be stepping outside of this manor."

"...I-I see..."

He had gotten worked up for nothing...

"First, we will gather the troops."

"I see..."

Mariel currently lived in the capital of Count Maslias's domain, which was located near a mountainous region. Mariel had arrived there with her butler and guards, wearing a top that had been specially ordered for her. The top was made so the talons of birds of prey wouldn't pierce through, with a protrusion sticking out of the shoulder area for them to perch on. And there perched a bird that wasn't considered a bird of prey.

"Okay then, please take care of it."

"Leave it to me, kaaaw!"

With that, the crow fluttered its wings energetically and flew away.

"And now, we wait."

"I-I see…"

That was all the butler could say…

One hour later.

"I scouted all of them, kaaaw!"

Lined up next to the crow were a hawk, an eagle, a falcon, a robin, a pigeon, a hummingbird, a parakeet, and many others…

"Splendid work! Please look forward to your special reward!"

"You mean that, Missy?! Ohh… I'll be able to let the little ones eat their fill for the first time in a while. Thanks, Missy… Kaaaw!"

Mariel cocked her head, wondering if the way the crow went out of its way to add "kaw" to the ends of its sentences was some sort of custom. She then left the crow to its emotional moment and went straight to talking about business. This was, of course, the discussion about the contracts of employment for the birds who had gathered there.

"…So, are we all in agreement regarding the terms? You will be getting food and treatment for injuries and illnesses for you and your families while in our employ. Regarding your treatment, we will do our best to accommodate your requests, but if it's beyond our capabilities, we must ask that you forgive us…"

"That's fine. Only a god can save one who is destined to die from their demise. If you will do what you can, and I can spend my final moments without hunger and in a warm place, that is more than I could ever hope for. To ask for more is arrogance, and disrespectful to the Goddess... Do you not agree?"

"Yes, I think so too."

The hawk and eagle, which seemed to have the highest authority, or rather, were positioned at the top of the pecking order out of all the birds that had arrived, so the others all nodded in agreement. The falcon, which seemed to be the strongest after the top two, stayed silent during the exchange.

In any case, Mariel had come to an agreement with the representatives of the birds. Now, each of those representatives should spread the word to their friends and send any willing participants to the manor.

"Thank you for coming. I am Mariel, the mistress of these children."

Mariel had returned to her villa and begun talking business to the stray dogs and pet dogs that her own canine soldiers had recruited. The terms of employment were pretty much the same as the birds, but some of the birds had an extra perk: they would get to send messages to their human friends who had taken care of them and fed them. Mariel had heard of this condition from her dogs after Kaoru had offered it to them.

Some of the dogs among them had participated in the impeachment of her uncle Aragorn, and thanks to them putting in a good word, the discussion went smoothly, without any issues.

"Yes, the preparations for vengeance are now complete! This time, we will have revenge, by our own hands, without troubling the Goddess for her help! We have already eliminated the mastermind behind the heinous crime, Aragorn. But I am not such a good person that I would be satisfied by his demise alone. Those who killed my father, mother, and brother for money… They still live without a care in the world. Did they really think I would turn a blind eye?"

Evil laughter.

Mariel had already finished crossing the river. The river that separated the innocent, cheerful, and bubbly aristocrat girl from the hardened, audacious seeker of revenge…

"These are the targets."

With that, Mariel pointed at four men who stepped out of a tavern. She had gathered information through judicious use of her money and had thus finally tracked down the Black Ops contact men.

"Please find out where they live, trail any allies they come in contact with, and take care of the other requested tasks. Big achievements will be handsomely rewarded with bonuses on top of your normal pay. For the bird troops, I will provide materials for your nests and shiny, pretty objects. For the dog army: chicken breasts, potatoes, or anything else you request. …And if you wish, I can take you in under our household's exclusive employment."

"Exclusive" in this case meant they would become her pet dogs. But being her pet didn't mean they would be leashed on a short chain all day. They were basically allowed to run loose, and could spend their free time however they wanted, as long as they patrolled the manor during their shift. A stable life where food and a roof over their heads was guaranteed… For the dogs who didn't have owners yet, this was a dream come true.

In fact, many of the dogs that already had owners were likely to switch over. After all, they would be able to communicate with their mistress if they moved in with Mariel. This meant they could tell her about their desires and troubles, and they would become kin to one who had received the love of the Goddess herself. Of course, this not only applied to the dogs, but the birds as well.

The groups of canine soldiers and bird troops let out cries of joy.

…As a side note, those were the names of the animal forces that Mariel had given them in order to differentiate them from House Raphael's own military forces. Among them were names like Crow Battalion and Falcon Squad.

"Falcons look strong, so they will be combat units. They seem like they would win no matter what, so they are the Let's Win Falcon Forces," Mariel said happily as she saw the cool-and-reliable-looking falcons.

The dogs and birds were ecstatic at her words, but she pressed a finger to her lips and signaled for silence, then gave out her command with her sharp voice.

"Our enemy is a criminal organization that murdered my family, known as Black Ops. Your mission is to crush them completely. I look forward to your success… Begin Operation Trash Cleanup!!!"

And so, the dogs and birds began tracking the men from a distance. Since it would soon become dark, the nocturnal birds like owls, nightjars, night herons, and snipes took the lead. Surprisingly, there weren't very many birds that couldn't see in the dark (besides chickens), and the majority of them could see pretty well even at night. It was just that not many of them flew during the night…

But this was just like how not many woodcutters and farmers worked at night, and it wasn't in any way strange for them to not do so. Who spread such a false rumor, anyway…? Regardless, it was best to let the specialists do what they were good at, so the nocturnal birds would take on the work at night.

One week later...

"The time has come..."

After trailing after the Black Ops members, the rest of their members and structure within the organization became clear, one after another. Normally, this would have been impossible. Everyone was cautious of people following them.

But who could have imagined this? The little birds resting on a tree branch and the dogs lying on the ground next to a shop were actually trailing their every step... They could slip through crowds, or escape through back doors, but it was impossible to shake off the birds watching from above or the dogs following their scent.

The members of Black Ops didn't necessarily know everyone else in the organization, and most of them only knew who they directly worked with, like their superiors, subordinates, or a couple of colleagues, other than the contact men who coordinated things. Those who had normal lives outside of the organization tried to avoid direct contact with other Black Ops members, and only met with the contact men.

...And one day, the contact men disappeared. All at once. Their throats were ripped out by wild dogs. They were poisoned by birds that had slipped something into their food. Their eyes were clawed out by hawks.

They couldn't reach their superiors. They couldn't reach their subordinates. They gradually lost contact with the rest of the organization, too... And one day, they were suddenly attacked by dogs and birds.

"What the hell is going on?! Why can't I reach my men?" shouted a man alone in his manor: The boss of Black Ops...or at least, he had been the boss.

He must have realized it too. He just didn't want to admit it. Indeed, the organization known as Black Ops no longer existed...

Most of those who had died lived in the criminal underworld, and nobody seemed to care if they suddenly went missing or if their bodies turned up. Because of this, they were often left where they had died, or thrown into garbage dumps or rivers, and treated as missing otherwise. After all, they had all suddenly died of causes like "attacked by a dog or wolf, or some sort of monster of that type," or "seemingly attacked by a bird-type monster."

Nobody cared about the strange deaths of the dregs of society. If anyone was moved by them, it may have been out of happiness. But sometimes, their deaths were reported to someone in Black Ops. Therefore, the fact that they were dying one after another had been relayed to the upper levels of the organization...but by that time, it was already too late. And at this point, the man who used to be the boss of Black Ops seemed to realize something.

"Dog or wolf-type monsters. Bird-type monsters. Only Black Ops members are attacked and killed..."

Those three words appeared in his head.

"B-Bitch Viscount. B-Bird Aristocrat... The request to attack House Raphael... D-Don't tell me..."

"...You wish to see me? No thank you, I have no desire to meet with a criminal..."

"...You resent being called a criminal when there's no proof? Then I will do my best not to leave any evidence, so I surely won't have to worry about being called a criminal myself."

"...You want me to stop? What in the world do you mean? Are you calling me a criminal without proof?"

"...Do you have any reason to believe I would do something to you? You don't? Then I obviously have no reason to do anything. Why did you come to me when you can't think of any such reason?"

Each time an emissary came to deliver a message, she made them return with simple replies.

Mariel didn't worry about the emissaries trying anything with her. No one could even think of laying a hand on her with dozens of dogs baring their fangs and dozens of birds of prey aiming to rip their eyes out.

And one day...

"Let us end this..."

The killer of her parents and brother had suffered long enough, living in constant fear of getting attacked at any moment.

"Tonight, we settle this."

"Awoooooooooo!!!"

"Scraaaaaaaaaw!!!"

That night, a single shadow stood in front of a certain criminal's manor.

"Thank you, everyone. It's now time for the final battle!"

"Woof, woof, woof! I'll stop that nasty smell once and for all!"

"Craaaw!"

And so, the girl stepped into enemy territory. Surrounded by dozens of dogs and dozens of birds flying overhead...

Afterword

Hello again, this is FUNA.

Thank you so much for reading volume 5 of *I Shall Survive Using Potions!* This time, Kaoru and friends are dragged into trouble and set out to strike back! They march into the capital and pick a fight with the aristocrats, Temple of the Goddess, and royal palace! The bonus story is all about Mariel! Has she fallen to the dark side?!

Kaoru: "Aristocrat girls are scary!"

And in volume 6 coming up, Kaoru faces danger and an unexpected sudden turn of events! Who could have seen it coming?! Thanks to all of your support, the next volume will be out…at least, it's planned to…I think…

This month (October 2019), volume 5 of the *Potions* novel, and from another publisher, *Didn't I Say to Make My Abilities Average in the Next Life?!* volume 12, volume 4 of the *Potions* manga, and volume 1 of a spin-off manga are planned for release, for a total of four books! …Sorry, this ended up being mostly an advertisement for another publisher.

And in October, the anime for *Didn't I Say to Make My Abilities Average in the Next Life?!* will be starting! I'm another step closer to fulfilling my ambitions…

The ongoing comic version is updated every first and third Monday on the webcomic magazine, "Suiyoubi no Sirius"! (http://seiga.nicovideo.jp/manga/official/w_sirius/)

To my editor, the illustrator Sukima, the binding designer, the proofreading supervisor, the publisher, distributor, bookstore workers, managers of the light novel publishing website, Shōsetsuka ni Narou, everyone who pointed out typos and gave advice and ideas in the comment section, and everyone who picked this book up, I am grateful from the bottom of my heart.

Thank you! I hope to see you again in the next volume...

FUNA

After her death, Kaoru was reincarnated in another world with cheat powers that allow her to create potions that can do anything she wants. When she uses them to help those in need, she naturally draws attention to herself. It isn't long before she's targeted by greedy men...

While all this is happening, someone sets their sights on Layette. Kaoru is enraged, but what will she decide to do...? All she wants is a peaceful potion-making life, but outside forces continue to keep her from her dream.

J-Novel Club LLC
www.j-novel.club